Before she and John had married, they had lain on the riverbank at Hampton Court or lolled about her apartment, reading together essays which John had marked: "The Proper Choice of Partners" and "Marriage as a Work of Art." They had proudly checked themselves against the requirements and agreed they were eminently suited to each other. They would talk all night, and her blood beat with the excitement of John's ideas. Who needed sleep?

And when dawn came, they would go out, she behind him on his Vespa, and they would streak across the bridge to a workingmen's cafe in Battersea. She would cling to him, her face against the rough sweater, her forehead just touching his dark shaggy hair.

A year ago, last spring.

Now they were in Majorca—vacationing. In her mirror, she saw herself, a disillusioned woman furiously brushing her hair, and the man with his back to her, bent frowning over his writing, and from the bed, the sharp wise eyes of his child, impassive, blue.

Other Novels
by
Gail Godwin

VIOLET CLAY

Published By
WARNER BOOKS

The Perfectionists

Gail Godwin

WARNER BOOKS

A Warner Communications Company

To
Kathleen Krahenbuhl Cole

Chapter
One

This island made her feel exposed. Its colors were raw and primeval: scalding azure sky, burnt sienna earth, leaves of dusty green. The scrutiny of its noon light rooted out the skulking shadow, the secret flaw, and measured these ruthlessly against the ideal. It pained them at first, the people coming from London, which was still sealed in the gloom of winter. They edged sidewise from the cool, dimly lit charter plane into the spotlight glare. They blinked, became conscious of their pallor.

Dane was suddenly reminded of the Orkin exterminator who came years ago to her father's house, back in the States. "Watch this," he told Captain Tarrant and his daughter. "I'm going to show you some real fun." And he crept in his white overalls and soft-soled shoes to the kitchen drawer, snatched it open with a blood-curdling yell and blazed his powerful flashlight upon a bunch of panicked roaches. "Ha!" he cried. "Look at the bastards go to pieces."

They went through customs. John first: Dr.

Empson, British subject. Bump-bump went the official stamp. "Yes, good," said the Majorcan customs officer. He had a neat moustache, dark liquid eyes and butterscotch-smooth skin. He gave John a respectful, guarded welcome. Dane was next. She handed him her American passport: Dane Tarrant Empson, while she got the little boy's ready.

Because of his special status, illegitimate son of Dr. Empson, in process of legal adoption by the doctor and his new wife, Robin had his own passport, although he was only three. The customs officer thought this was odd. He gave Dane, whom he assumed to be the child's mother, a puzzled look, tinctured with sex. The little boy he chucked affectionately under the chin.

"*Hermoso*," he said. "Can you smile?"

The child regarded him with cool blue eyes and did not smile. Penelope came last: British passport. "Miss MacMahon. V*ery* good." Bump-*bump*. The stamp gave a little lilt to the red-gold hair, the country cheeks of Britain.

"He was nice," Penelope said to Dane as they went along to the baggage area. "The way they look at you here. A lovely greedy look that men never let show in England."

"Mmm," said Dane. She thought about greedy men not for the first time recently. The little boy clung to her hand as impersonally as if it had been a towrope.

John said, "No use for you people to follow me through this crush. Why don't you wait here by the front entrance; I can manage the bags." He went off, a tall heavyset man in a dark wool suit. His slight limp gave him a certain arrogance. He'd had polio at twelve. One leg was thinner than the other, the arch of that foot deformed. Robin detached himself from Dane's hand and ran off after his father.

"Serious little soul, isn't he?" Penelope said. "I wonder what he thinks of all this. Never been in an airplane before, brand-new country and all. Won't this be the first time he's really away from the Christophers?"

"Yes, we've only taken him for weekends so far. This is his big transition. When we get back to London, he'll stay with us during the week and visit the foster home on weekends. That's John's way of making a slow break for him. Mrs. Christopher's a wonderful mother, probably better than I will ever be."

"Nonsense," said Penelope. "You've so much more to offer him. Why, he even looks like you. Gosh, what strange luck you had. I wish *I* could go to a new country to work and within a year find a brilliant man who wanted to marry me and a ready-made little son who had my eyes and didn't even have to have his diapers changed anymore. Oh dear." She sighed. Thinking no doubt about her own unattachment. "I love John," she went on. "He has saved me from utter despair. It was so kind of you both to ask me on your holiday. Kind in the way most people can't manage, I think."

"Don't be silly. We wanted you," Dane assured her, which was true. Especially in her

9

own case. Dane liked having Penelope around because of the way Penelope saw her marriage, her life.

"You know, I was writing Mum and Dad about it. About my being John's patient and all. That would have made a difference to most doctors. Their professional thing. But John is above all that, I told them. He's not *conventional*."

"No, he's certainly not conventional," replied Dane with a bitter little laugh.

John came back alone, carrying the bags.

"Where's Robin?" he asked.

"He went with you. I thought you saw him," Dane said.

"Yes! We saw him run along with you, to get the luggage," chimed in Penelope, and Dane felt unreasonably grateful to her.

"I see," John said, beginning to go dark. He bestowed a grave and disappointed look on the two women. "I expect he's lost, then. Penelope, would you mind looking over there for him?" He pointed toward the busy portion of the hall, where clusters of new arrivals were gathered round tour leaders who addressed them in English, French and German. Penelope nodded, bit her lip, plunged into the Babel like a guilty child.

"I'll go back to the baggage claim," John said, carefully keeping any accusation out of his tone. She'd rather he'd said, "Damn it to hell, why couldn't you keep an eye on him!" But that was not John's way. "You'd best remain here," he said, "in case he finds his way back to you." He turned away from her, shouldering purposefully back toward Baggage, his face tense and abstracted.

Dane stood at her post by the open door and frowned into this piercingly bright sun. John would see her letting Robin get lost as a symbolic thing. Beyond the implications of losing the child were the more serious ones of losing John as a child. For, he had often told her, Robin was himself as a child. Also, John saw himself as a collection of selves, some of which had grown faster than others. The parts which were still developing—his "tender growing parts" he called them—she was to nourish, tend and encourage, in order to make him a whole man. Penelope thought she was a lucky woman. Maybe she was, maybe she was, but it was all so difficult and tiring.

Cabbies were organizing their fares outside in the parking area for journeys to various points of the island. "Arenal!" called one. "Main 'otels een Palma!" shouted another. Swarthy, hefty-bellied men. (Lately she'd been dreaming of Negroes, Mayflower Van moving men.) The cabbies sweated as they tossed fine leather suitcases onto the roof racks of their cabs with cheerful disregard for their welfare over the first bumpy road. She and John and Penelope and Robin were going to a place called Cala d'Or, on the eastern side of the island. She had chosen it herself from a brochure. Shying away from pictures of the spacious, open beaches alive with international youth and beauty, she had pounced at once on the small, secluded spot. Nestled in its cove, surrounded by a shield of dark pines, possessed of a private beach, the austere whitewashed hotel had called to her own needs. She saw it as a place to recover balance and confidence in herself, a place to swim and grow beautiful again in her own private mirror, unchallenged by comparison with the really beautiful, the really vigorous. . . . She wanted to fall in love with her husband under the sun, to feel herself lucky, to cope brilliantly with the child, to excite the envy of some few others and to feel alive, really alive.

Robin had never spoken to her. Not one word during the whole ten months she had been married to John.

For some minutes, she had been staring at a pale, wraith-like woman reflected in the glass of the open door of the customs building. Now she realized that this was, unfortunately, herself. The short helmetlike haircut she'd thought so sleekly boyish all winter made her look sharp as a shrew in this light. The light-blue eyes squinted back at her through a network of tiny lines. The winter has made me old, she thought, and grimaced and looked away.

John led the child back, stooping in order to reach the boy's hand. "Well, I found him," he said, unsmiling. Robin's face, a miniature of John's heavy-featured, dark-browed one, was puckered and red as a little grape. The eyelashes of the blue eyes, which were now bloodshot, had separated into wet little starpoints. He looked up at her as though she had failed him.

"He was over by the baggage, trapped in

that mob, crying his heart out," John said. "Some ugly woman was trying to comfort him, only frightening him all the more." Dane knew from the way his face went suddenly soft and pouty that he was being himself as a neglected child, back in Cairo or Burma or Vancouver, lonely and misunderstood by a financier father who thought only of making money and an ineffectual mother.

"I'm sorry," she began. "I had no idea—"

Penelope burst back onto the scene. "You've found him! Oh thank goodness!" She went down on her knees to touch the boy's face. He turned it away from her. She stood up again, rather embarrassed.

"Shall we find ourselves a taxi, now we're all together again, and go along to our spot?" John said. He bequeathed his son's stiff hand to Dane's care, picked up the three big bags and the small one and led the way to the parking area.

In the taxi, Penelope pressed avidly forward in her seat and thrust firm round arms out of her sleeveless cotton frock. She looked as though she might take a bite out of the island any minute. The taxi accelerated, gaily bumping them over the rough roads, past red dirt farms and gawking, sinister cactus plants, some high as humans. "Look, windmills!" she cried. "Every farm has its own little windmill." She turned to John. "You know," she confided, "my depression thing seems to have gone. Just since we landed on this island."

John had been staring straight ahead,

deep in thought, his lips moving slightly as his long fingers made patterns in the space above his lap, a habit which had intrigued Dane at the very beginning and now gave her the creeps. He came out of his thoughts, smiled rather charmingly at Penelope and said, "I am glad. I think we underestimate the personalities of places. I think they can influence us as deeply as people do. They were here long before we were and they will be here after we've gone."

One of Dane's original reasons for wanting him was precisely this sort of remark. It set weird resonances working in her.

"That's true," said Penelope, looking enlightened.

Then John noticed Dane. He looked at her as though he'd just remembered something nice. "Hello," he said, reaching over and taking her hand. He caressed it thoughtfully with his thumb. He seemed to have forgotten all about his recently lost child, who sat rigidly on her lap. Then suddenly, shored up by her reality, he went opaque once more, returned to his abstractions. His moist dark eyes behind the glasses withdrew into privacy. He faced front, as if he'd heard a summons.

The child couldn't be comfortable, sitting far out on the edge of her lap. Besides, he was hurting her knees. Experimentally she lowered them. He gave a little grunt and whirled around to accuse her with the blue eyes. Okay. She put her legs back in the uncomfortable position. He rearranged himself grudgingly and turned away again. She allowed herself a fully orchestrated moment of pique toward Robin Andrew Empson, at the same time enjoying a little her own martyrdom.

Penelope plunged into her straw bag and brought out the island brochure which she had worn to shreds since Dane gave it to her. She turned to a familiar page and read aloud: "'Cala d'Or: Sequestered in a charming cove at the southeast tip of this popular Balearic Isle, Cala d'Or provides a quiet and natural setting for a special breed of tourist. . . .'"

Penelope had broken down in Barclay's Bank because a clerk had told her she'd forgotten to date her check. She had gone into a fit of sobs and the manager had gently sent her home in a taxi. She slept with the overhead light on and had hired men come in to remove her closet doors after she had heard mournful sighs coming repeatedly from within. She had been a perfect jittery wreck when she'd first come to John several months ago. He had made her better. He had that rare talent of explaining people to themselves, computerizing their shadowy miasmas in his great brain and handing them back a neat card on which their secrets and fears had been programmed into a coherent, less threatening shape. Penelope was not crazy; she had been lonely to the point of despair, simply. Impervious London turned a noncommittal eye on one more bright and hopeful girl of middle-class background, arriving from Yorkshire in search of her future. She'd waited four years, clerking in Hatchard's bookshop, for this future to begin. ("It's no wonder she's hearing things in her closets,"

Dane had told John. ("I'd be hoping for things in mine.") If Penelope had been American, from the same background, she would have got a scholarship to her state university and spent her four years waiting there, instead of clerking in a bookstore. But the daughter of an English tech-school master and a mother who sent John brown paper parcels of home-grown runner beans through the post had no such opportunity in England. She always came too early for her sessions with John. Dane had got into the habit of inviting her up for coffee. They would talk, like any two girls. Penelope envied Dane's marriage and thought her "cool." Dane secretly admired Penelope's greater vitality. So Penelope had herself a friend in the unfriendly city, and Dane was allowed the small luxury of knowing her own circumstances, far from agreeable to herself, coveted by someone else.

Robin shifted dictatorially on her legs. Her dress was completely crushed. The taxi passed through a fresher, cooler landscape studded with plants and trees of a deeper green. Often she imagined what Robin's first words to her would be: Mommy? No? I want that? Go to hell? Impassive little god, his snobbery crushed her, fascinated her. She studied him under this new light, hoping to see, suddenly, just another child. But his cool little face was just the same with bright sun pouring in on it: utterly impassive. He was three, but his uncannily mature features made him appear wise and rather censorious of the world's ways.

He did not look at all like the real mother, John had assured her, as if that made everything all right.

"You are the perfect mother for Robin," he would say with finality, as though he'd planned it all, this perfect match. But Dane wanted all the facts, photos, memories to assemble for herself, and make her own meaning of her husband's interlude with this other woman. What color had *her* eyes been, for instance? John said he honestly didn't remember. Were they the same ice blue as Robin's? As Dane herself had such eyes, what an enormous consolation it would have been to find that the real mother's eyes had been brown or gray or purple! Her name was Vanessa. (Dane always thought of Vanessa Redgrave and was miserable.) She and John had worked together as doctors in a county hospital, shortly after they'd both qualified.

"For God's sake, don't you have any pictures?" Dane would ask. No pictures. Well, was she tall, did she resemble me, was she pretty—prettier? Quite pretty, he thought, not too tall, rather plump. A natural country girl. She'd been brought up with horses and loved to ride. "How plump?" Not disagreeably so, no, just robust, healthy. "Did you love her?" Dane was thin and rather sallow in the winter; she had always been a mess at sports. Love? He pondered. There was certainly affection, and a physical closeness. But Vanessa had been content with such a very small part of him, she hadn't been able to perceive him all, so how could there be love, at its deepest level? Had they married, Vanessa would ultimately have felt degraded, because she couldn't, didn't have the capacity to, share all of his universes. "Can I?" "You're capable of doing so," he replied. "That is why I married you." Dane entertained private thoughts of meeting Vanessa for lunch, making friends with her, finding out her weaknesses and her strengths. She wanted the girl in their life, somehow. But Vanessa was gone. Soon after the child was born and John still would not marry her, she made a clean break. Leaving the child in the hands of the foster mother and her lawyers, she emigrated to Canada and was practicing medicine there.

Before Dane married John, he took her to the foster home to meet his son. She moved reverently toward the withdrawn child sitting passively in the window seat, one leg tucked under him on the cushion, as if he were holding his own court. He wore a red-and-white sailor suit, had long ash-brown curls and looked exactly like a storybook child. She held out to him, as one might approach a shy animal, a cardboard cylinder of Smarties, the same sweets John always brought for his once-a-week visits.

"Hello, Robin," she said. "I'm Dane. I've brought you some Smarties."

He did not react at all, only watched her impartially from his chintz-cushioned window seat like some ancient, silent king.

John hovered behind her. "Don't worry," he said. "It's bound to take a while. Let me." And adroitly he edged past her and seated himself beside the child on the window seat. He lifted him into his lap. "Well, hello there," he said sociably in his best doctor's manner. The child did not offer a flicker of response, but let himself be held. For some moments they sat, posed like an old-fashioned photograph. The boy was almost a physical copy of the man. She sat down on the flowered carpet and observed the two of them sitting formally above her. Mrs. Christopher had allotted them her sacred "front room" for this important meeting. "You'll not be disturbed," said the good woman, smelling of milk and ironing. She had raised one hundred and eight foster children, she told Dane proudly. And six of her own as well.

"Give me the Smarties," John said from the window seat. Obediently Dane handed over her gift and John offered it to the boy. He took it greedily and began prying with his fingers at the plastic lid.

"Let me help him." She started forward, crawling toward the window seat.

"No, he'll do it by himself. Watch: how he works it out like a problem. There. He's got it."

"Bring him down on the floor," she suggested.

The two adults crouched on the flowery carpet beside the regal child. He sat sideways, both legs tucked under him, and went at the Smarties with a special system. First he pried off the lid. Then he peeked inside the box and extracted one colored sweet, which he immediately concealed in his fist. Then he closed the box and popped the Smarty quickly, furtively, into his mouth, chewing it in even little crunches between the small and perfect teeth. In the act of swallowing it, he began prying off the lid for the second Smarty.

"He's resourceful, isn't he?" said Dane, repelled by the ungenerous little ritual.

"Don't you think he's fascinating to watch?" said John. "Oh, *thank* you, Robin," for the child had offered his daddy a brown Smarty. John popped it into his mouth with the same quick, greedy motion as the child. "Want to offer Mommy one?" he asked, munching.

The child closed the box.

But she had continued to court him respectfully. She had long discussions in Mrs. Christopher's kitchen while John took the boy for walks. Dane liked Mrs. Christopher. She found her so reassuring. Also, she hoped to find out more about Vanessa.

"He's always been a quiet child, understand," Mrs. Christopher said. She was giving a little black baby his bottle. He had been abandoned in a pushcart in a Sainsbury's market. "I mean, ever since he can remember, Robin hasn't known for certain where to hang his hat. He's been with me ever since he was born, but he's been told that someday he's to go and live at his *real* home with his father, see. Now that may sound simple to us, but a child can't comprehend so well. Oh, I don't mind telling you, I kept hoping they'd marry, just for *his* sake, you know. But it wasn't to be—" The Negro infant spit milk down the front of Mrs. Christopher's dress. "Now what do you want to do that for? Eh?" Good-naturedly she wiped it away with a cloth, joggling the baby all the while. "Poor John. I know he's done the best he can, considering, coming out regularly to see him, always generous about money for his little clothes and things. It's difficult when you're a doctor and have patients. But now he's got you. When John wrote that you and him were getting married, do you know what I did? I got down on my knees, right there with the washing machine going, and thanked God that John had found the right woman at last. I kept askin' him for the longest time, see, 'When are you going to find a nice girl and settle down?' after *she* left, and he'd say, 'When I find the *right* one, Mrs. Christopher.' He was particular, all right. But now he's got you and do you know: Robin looks more like you than he did *her!* That's the truth. Your eyes are the same, exactly the same. It's uncanny. As if you was meant—Everybody's going to think he's your own."

"He's never said anything," Dane began. "Does he—"

"Oh, he talks. Not much to adults, mind you, though of course he talks to me when he wants something or often when we're alone. But I've heard him give right sharp orders to the other children when they're playing in the garden. Don't worry, dear. It's bound to take time. He's got to be certain of you first. It's his sort of little test, don't you see. It was ever so long before he took any notice of John, only don't say I said it. He'll come round. Just give him lots of love. Lots of love is what he needs."

The months passed, with tedious twice-weekly drives to the foster home in Croydon. They were married now. Winter was coming and it grew dark very early. They drove past factories and county council housing to pick up sullen Robin and take him back to John's house in London for the afternoon. John bought elaborate educational toys from Galt's and arranged them on the divan for Robin to see as soon as he came in. The child always went immediately to the divan, a greedy frown on his face, to see what they'd got him this time. Dane felt they were politicians trying to win his uncertain vote. Sometime in the past, John had established a limited number of communicative routines with the child. These never varied from week to week—the Smarty routine, from which Dane was still excluded, and some acrobatics. John would, for instance, swing the boy dangerously high in the air and Robin would widen his eyes and make his mouth into a big O and look relieved when he was back on the ground. Or John would get down on the floor and cringe like a dog while Robin beat him him energetically with his fists. Oh, oh, ohhh, John would howl, as if in great pain.

When Robin began coming to them for weekends, they hovered nervously about him, offering him this and that tidbit. Some he accepted, others he rejected. There was no way of knowing. He ate Smarties constantly and wet the bed every night. Often Dane would tiptoe into his room to feel the sheets and would find him lying there in the dark, eyes wide open, but apparently asleep.

Very rarely, he spoke to his father. Never if she was in sight. Once she hid outside the living room and peeked through a crack in the door. He sat on John's knee, his rigid small back to her. Both father and son seemed in a sort of trance as they looked out of the window. Suddenly he said softly:

"Look . . . Dad-dy . . . out dere . . . a big tree. It has . . . uh . . . fwowers on it." The voice was halting, mechanical, like a talking doll's—a talking cockney doll. It was crippled already with the Christophers' cockney vowels. The discrepancy between that aloof little body and those lower-class sounds gave Dane a strange thrill.

"That's right!" came John's pleased reply. "Those are *leaves*. Say 'leaves.' Can you say 'leaves' . . . 'leaves'?" But the child said nothing else.

One Saturday evening when John was below, sorting files in his office, Dane deliberately held off Robin's supper until she knew he must be hungry. Then she took him on her lap, smiled gently and said, "Robin, are you hungry?"

He looked at her.

"Robin," she said a bit more sharply, "I asked you were you hungry. Can you say something? Then you can have your supper." But he only looked at her curiously, as if she must play out this game with herself while he waited for his supper. Finally she gave up, defeated, and went to prepare his boiled egg on toast. He followed her to the kitchen, stepping along lightly within her movements as she made the late supper.

She began hating him a little. She had satisfying visions of beating him. She conjured up images of his red, enraged face acknowledging her, at last, in his pain. He was small and at her mercy. She imagined him below her, screaming with rage and fear, and got a pleasurable feeling in her stomach.

She let her imagination dwell on folk tales of changelings and children inhabited by evil spirits. Robin's profile grew sharper each week when they went to collect him from the home. He was so unchildlike in appearance, his rigid little body proportioned like a man's. A perfect little shrunken man. The blue eyes, cool and critical, followed her everywhere, but always just skirted acknowledging her. She read in a psychology book that a person could be driven mad by lack of acknowledgment, somebody consistently denying your reality. Flipping one day through her college anthology of French poetry, she came across Rimbaud's poem about the child with blue eyes who, wise beyond his years, regarded his mother with loathing and condescension:

*Dans les yeux bleus et sous le front plein
  d'éminences
L'âme de son enfant livrée aux repugnances . . .*

"Read this," she told John. "A child can't feel like that."

"Yes," he said. "I felt that way myself. I remember it perfectly. We were living in Cairo then. I was less than a year old. It was a hot afternoon and I was lying in my cot and my father was hitting me on the face again and again because I had been crying and woke him from his nap. My mother was standing beside him saying, 'Don't, Vivian, please don't hit the baby,' but she was afraid to interfere. Even while I was yelling, I thought: Silly woman, *you're* no good to me at all. I'm on my own."

"You can't remember something that happened when you were less than a year old, John."

"Yes I can. The only reason people forget is because they want to. If we were all clear, with no aberrations, we could remember everything, before we were born, even. I wonder what Robin will grow up to be. He's so complex. Don't you wonder?"

"I do wonder."

Chapter
Two

Their taxi lurched into a clean little village
and began to slow. They passed a bar called
Pedro's. Tourists in various stages of tanning
lounged about round tables of bright colors,
drinking from iced glasses. Directly across the
street, Spanish people were coming out of Sunday mass from a gaunt, gray church. Dane
counted three kinds of women: the young and
virginal, with their white missals and fresh
skins; the married and pregnant; and the old
and widowed, draped in funeral black. She
envied them their definitive stages of woman-
hood. It was all done for them. They had only
to flow along with nature's seasons, being
courted, bedded, bechilded and bereaved.
There were not all those interstices of ambition and neurosis for them to fall into.

The taxi turned into a dirt road and
bounced along under the shade of great pine
trees. Suddenly, there was a somber white
hotel, heavily shaded with pines. The taxi went
into its circular drive and stopped. There was

complete stillness. The hotel might have been uninhabited.

"Here we are," said John.

"But where's the sea?" said Dane, sure they had been cheated.

"Oh, I think I can smell it," said Penelope. "It's surely round back."

They all got out.

"Um, *cuánto cuesta?*" John asked the driver.

"One hundred fifty pesetas," said the driver, rather aggressively. "This is forty kilo from the airport." While waiting for John to sort through unfamiliar Spanish currency, he set his black beret at a jauntier angle, turned his back on them and whistled a popular tune.

A dapper man resembling an Arthur Murray dance teacher clicked down the front steps of the hotel. He wore a black suit and highly polished black shoes with absurdly pointed toes. He had a trim dark moustache.

"Doctor, señora, I have been expecting you. And señorita. Welcome to the Hotel Cala d'Or I am Ramírez-Suárez, manager. Ah, *què bonito,* what a beautiful child. Look how straight he stands!" Ramírez-Suárez flung himself to one knee in front of the child and opened his heart. "What is your name?" he implored.

Robin stepped back. He stared aloofly through the manager.

"His name is Robin," Dane said. "He's awfully shy with new people. You mustn't mind." But she was sad for him, knowing how

Spaniards adored children. Now he probably felt a failure.

"Oh, is all right," said Ramírez-Suárez, getting to his feet. "I understand. New place, new faces. I am sure he would love a Coca-Cola. I have them send up from the bar with my compliments." He regarded the child wistfully.

"No, please don't bother," Dane said.

"Is no bother, señora. It is my pleasure."

They all tramped upstairs. The hotel was cool and rather bare. The walls were a simple whitewashed stucco and the only adornments were the mosaic tile floors and enormous green potted plants. The Empsons' room was on the top floor. Ramírez-Suárez led the way, holding sadly aloft in one hand the sweating Coca-Cola which Robin had refused. Penelope and John followed, and Dane brought up the rear, held back by Robin, who had to put both feet on each stair.

On the second landing, the top of his Smarties box fell off. He had doggedly clutched this box during the taxi trip. Now multicolored Smarties spattered everywhere, raining down on the tiles like thousands of small explosions. The boy's unbelieving eyes tried to cope with this deluge, keep track of each absconding Smarty, but it was too much for him. He went deathly pale, then began reddening. He let out an unearthly scream and began running round and round in a circle, his head tucked between his shoulders. The heel of his brown oxford caught a candy here and there and ground its soft center into the tiles.

Dane dropped to the floor frantically and began picking up the Smarties. If only he would stop, if only he would stop.

Two curious maids appeared in the doorway of a room. One held a mop. Dane gathered the pellets and dropped them—*pok, pok, pok*—into the cardboard cylinder which Robin had flung down in despair. His scream subsided to a whimper. She found the lid of the box and snapped it firmly into place. "There," she said. "See? They're all back again."

He wouldn't accept the box. Still whimpering, he stared hard at her, then pointed a stiff little finger toward a large potted palm.

"There's another one beneath that palm, it seems," John said. They all watched while Dane crawled on her hands and knees behind the plant and retrieved the final Smarty. She placed this with exaggerated care into the box, closed it again and handed it to Robin with a thin smile.

"See, *hermosito*, your candies have all return," said Ramírez-Suárez, tweaking his moustache at the boy. Gaily he turned and led them up the final flight of stairs.

The first thing Dane saw were the two single beds covered with clean white cotton spreads. She felt oddly relieved. Ramírez-Suárez hurried ahead of them into the room, flung back French doors and let in a flood of light.

"Here is your balcony!" he announced proudly. They all followed him onto the spacious balcony. The small private beach was down below. The green sea stretched beyond the little cove. A mile or more from the beach was a tiny island with a yellow ruined fortress covering almost all of it.

"Oh, what is that fort?" John asked.

"Is pretty old," said Ramírez-Suárez, nodding wisely toward it.

"About how old would you say?" John pressed him. "The Inquisition, perhaps?"

Ramírez-Suárez pondered, then said, "Yes, I think. The Inquisition." He looked immensely pleased when John brightened.

"We might swim out," John said to his wife. "We might find something interesting."

"Yes." She looked down at the people on the beach. "How lovely and brown some of them are," she remarked. "I hope I can get like that."

"They are just mad, those people," said Ramírez-Suárez. "They try and get cooked all at one time. Very foolish at the hottest part of the day."

"True," said John. They went inside, out of the sun.

"The lunch is being serve, any time when you are ready," said the manager. "Shall I show you your room now, señorita? It is without *balcón,* but is much cooler in the day. And, Doctor, I have put a cot in the room. The little boy is with señorita, did not you arrange that?"

"That's right," said John. "Miss MacMahon and the boy will share a room. I'd better go along, to help him settle in."

"Come on, Robin Redbreast. Let's go and see *our* room," Penelope said cheerfully. She tried to take his hand.

The boy's face darkened. He would not move.

"Come along, Robin," John said. "Don't you want to see your room?"

Robin began stamping his feet. His face went redder and redder as the little brown shoes beat on the floor. He glared at the adults, who stood in a circle around him, and a noise like a siren warming up came from his throat.

"None of that," John said firmly, "or I shall have to spank you."

"You know what I think?" offered Ramírez-Suárez. "He does not want to leave his mother. That is natural." He looked respectfully and anxiously at the stamping child. "I think he is unaccustom to the new place, but will soon be all right."

"Oh hell," said Dane. She went out on the balcony by herself, leaving a wake of silence in which they dealt with her abruptness. Then she heard Ramírez-Suárez say softly, "The journey from London is exhausting for you, I know. Maybe, I tell you, we put a little cot in this room, just for a few days, until he gets accustom to the new place."

Let them settle it however they chose. Anchored by the heavy bright heat, she closed her eyes and ears and let it press her down. *Let* the sun bake her senseless in the hottest part of the day. Let it broil her brain free of all complexities. Let it burn her back into the same earth which held the bones of ancient peasants and the decayed petals of bygone flowers. She did not wish to compete, or to understand or to participate anymore. After ten months of this mentally and spiritually exhausting marriage, she wanted to be just a body— left alone. She felt tight in the head, like something was growing—a flower someone planted in a pot too small. She envied those Spanish women coming out of the church.

John came out on the balcony. "We've decided to move a cot for him into our room, temporarily," he said. His tall form cast a shadow between her and the sun. "Are you all right?" He was studying her, she knew.

"I'm sorry about the tantrum," she said. "I was so depressed. First losing him like that, then the hot drive, then those damn Smarties going all over the place . . . The scene in the room finished it. God, children are a responsibility."

"We can manage together," he said. "How are you feeling about things now?"

"Oh, better. As long as you'll talk to me. I can't bear it when you go abstracted. I'm always afraid you're mad at me. I'm sorry about losing Robin."

"That's fine," he said, smoothing her short hair with his fingers. He always said "That's fine" when she unburdened herself to him, gave him new and valuable clues to the whereabouts of more of those troublesome symptoms that linger quietly in the shadows of the personality, like insects under rocks. "Robin will be less of a problem when he begins to feel at home with us."

"Why don't you take off that old wool suit

and get into your holiday clothes?" she said. She imagined him with a tan. His body wasn't bad, if he would take care of it. He seemed often to forget he had one; forgot to shave or brush his teeth or comb his hair. She had to remind him and then they fought over it. At other times, he dramatized his body. They would be listening to a symphony in the living room when suddenly he would rise and begin to move about the room, swaying his hands and arms. an ecstatic faraway look in his eyes. She couldn't bear this; she always left the room. When they made love, he kept his eyes open. He would look at her intensely, his whole consciousness intruding between her and the oblivion she wanted to feel.

They returned to the room, her arm linked in his. The two maids who had watched the Smarty performance were making up Robin's cot. As they tucked in the sheets, they cast affectionate side-glances at Robin, who stood vigilant over their labor.

"*Hola, hermoso! Mira, Elena: sus ojos! Qué azules!*"

He frowned at them.

"It's going to be crowded in here," Dane remarked dryly. John, misinterpreting her, put his arm around her. His woolen sleeve was hot and scratchy on her bare neck.

"Listen," he said, "I have an idea. He can sleep in here. We can take our mattresses outside on the balcony and sleep under the stars."

He sounded so pleased at the prospect of this new venture into physicality. But she felt herself go cold.

"No, I wouldn't like it," she said.

"Why not?"

"I couldn't sleep in the open. I never have been able to."

He said, "You never used to worry about sleeping. Remember when we once talked all night and went out to breakfast at dawn? Then you would go to work. Before we married. And for some time after. You never complained about sleep." The brown eyes had started to plead with her behind the National Health glasses. His face became eager, boyish. He let her see how much it meant to him and she revolted, she couldn't help herself.

"We ought to go down to the dining room," she said. "Robin hasn't eaten anything since we left London. He refused the sweet roll on the plane."

He turned away from her, heaved his suitcase onto one of the single beds and began to unpack his things. He was not invulnerable, nobody was, she knew that. Only why did his weaknesses and vulnerabilities have to repel her so?

"I'm sorry," she said. "Look, I'm just as aware as you are that something is wrong between us."

The maids had slipped quietly from the room. Robin had not moved from his spot. Now he watched the adults, turning his face toward one and then the other, as if he understood everything.

Dane sat down on the other bed and sighed loudly. She wished she could crawl under

34

the sheet and go to sleep. "Look," she said, "you say I shouldn't lie about things. You say you want total truth between us. So I let you know my truth and it hurts you. What do you want me to do?"

"Don't attack the tender shoots of me," he said. "The parts that are growing and vulnerable. Every time I expose them to you, you do your best to murder them."

She hated it when he talked this way. "Tender shoots of me." It set her teeth on edge. She began picking at the white bedspread; she couldn't look at him.

"I know such talk infuriates you," he went on. "I can see it in your face. But you're my wife. If I can't expose myself to you, then to whom? I know you would like it if I stayed in my doctor-protector role all of the time. When the unintegrated, blundering little boy peeps out, it threatens you. But unless he comes out, he will *remain* unintegrated and blundering."

"Oh, stop it!" she cried. "Do you think I want to feel the way I feel? I know I'm intolerant. I want to love all of you so that the goddamn unintegrated parts will straighten themselves out. Don't you think I want to? But something rises up in me and turns me off. Is it my fault?" She took her hairbrush from her purse and marched to the mirror and began brushing her hair passionately, tearing at her scalp.

"I wish I could do it by myself," he said, laying out stacks of underclothes and socks, two terry cloth shirts he'd bought for the holiday, neither in colors she liked, a rust and a drab olive. "Perhaps I can. But then I wouldn't need you."

"Oh, need!" Her pale angry face sizzled with hair. Her head was on fire. She brushed on, harder, hurting herself. Now he was unpacking his pads of foolscap and his books. She watched him in the mirror. Out came his heavily underlined Yeats, kept from his Oxford days, and Count Hermann Keyserling's *Book of Marriage*, which he renewed again and again from the Westminister library. Essays on marriage by all the Count's famous friends: Jung, Adler, Thomas Mann . . . Only Bernard Shaw had refused to write one, explaining to the Count, who quoted him in the preface, that he did not dare tell the truth about marriage, at least while his wife was still living.

Before she and John had married, they had lain on the riverbank at Hampton Court, or lolled about her apartment, reading together the essays which John had marked: "The Proper Choice of Partners," "Marriage as a Psychological Relationship," "Correct Statement of the Marriage Problem," and "Marriage as a Work of Art." They had proudly checked themselves against the requirements and agreed they were eminently suited to each other. The old black book which nobody else ever seemed to want, with its mixture of illuminating and impenetrable passages, had been a metaphor for their courtship. It went with the all-night conversations in her flat overlooking the river, when her blood beat with the excitement of John's ideas. Their conversations resounded in the unexplored caverns of her mind. She had felt as though she were being transformed. Who needed sleep?

And when dawn came, it always amazed her. *Their* consciousness had bridged the sedatives of night. The dawn seemed proof they would go on talking forever. They would go out then, she would climb behind him on his Vespa, and they would streak across the bridge to a workingmen's café in Battersea. She would cling to him, her face against the rough sweater, her forehead just touching his dark shaggy hair. As they came off the bridge, there was a sudden sharp turning to the left, and she keened her body with his to make the turn.

A year ago, last spring. Baked beans and fried eggs and good coffee in crude white mugs. Surrounded by workmen. The day beginning and they're going to get married and continue like this for forty or fifty more years and never stop discovering.

In the mirror, beyond the disillusioned woman furiously brushing her hair and the man with his back to her, bent frowning over his task, were the sharp wise eyes of the child, impassive, blue.

Chapter Three

They were the last to lunch in the dining room, a bright porched-in room with pots of geraniums on the ledges and a view of the sea. For dessert, there was no longer the choice listed on the menu of flan, ice cream or peaches. Only peaches.

John leaned toward his son, who was enthroned on three pillows Ramírez-Suárez had snatched from the lounge. "Would you like to bathe in the sea, Robin?" he asked.

"Oh, that would be fun! Wouldn't it!" Penelope encouraged.

The child nodded once, solemnly, to his father.

"I'll take him up and get him ready," said Dane, downing the remainder of her wine. "I'm ready to go myself."

"Oh dear," said John. "Who will stay and have coffee with me?"

"I will. You promised to tell me about ESP," said Penelope.

"If you like," he said, looking pleased.

Dane lifted Robin from his pillows and

set him on the floor. "Come with Mommy." The words sounded awkward. But she had to start sometime. She led him away. John poured coffee for Penelope and himself and began explaining his resonance theory of extrasensory perception, which had been Dane's introduction to him.

He had been sitting in an armchair, half in shadow, speaking to a group of intellectuals. They were Mensa people, the high-IQ society. Dane was doing clubs for the society magazine she worked for. A Mensa meeting was no news to such a magazine, but old Lady Jane Rotherhall, who happened to be a member, was. The meeting was being held at her Bloomsbury Square town house.

Dane arrived late, pleasantly high from her previous assignment at the Dorchester: an annual get-together of a horse breeders' society. Having dined and drunk with cheerful, ruddy outdoor types, she was not looking forward to a pallid, cerebral little gathering—and a speech to listen to. Lady Jane, an elderly spinister in a drab hostess gown, met her at the door. "I'm afraid the speaker has begun," she said, leading her on tiptoe toward the drawing room, where a dozen or so middle-aged people sat in a circle around a man in an armchair, a dark-haired man in his thirties. "Dr. Empson is some sort of psychiatrist," Lady Jane whispered. "He is speaking about ESP. Fascinating. Oh dear, I'm afraid there are no chairs left."

"I don't mind sitting on the floor," said Dane.

"You don't? Really? Well, go up front, at least."

Dane, feeling rather bold in this drab group, slipped easily through the chairs and dropped to the rug at his feet. He looked down at her with mild curiosity just as he was saying, "Couldn't our memories be a form of telepathy—with our selves of yesterday?"

He spoke in a low, persuasive voice, like a father or a teacher instructing children. His voice was years older than he was. There was something different about him. His craggy features, which could have been bucolic on another, were charged with a zealous, sensitive energy. His black hair had the carelessly combed look of a genius. His dark liquid eyes snapped and glistened from behind his glasses with the fire of one who has seen, and come back from, a vision.

For a long time, Dane had been on the lookout for, if not an actual vision, at least an event charged with meaning which would signal the turning point of her life. Not only would she recognize it intellectually, but her very guts should respond to it. Like Jacob's angel, it would jostle her to her core and she would be transformed. She had expected the loss of virginity to be such a thing; but it had carried no more "charge" than having her tooth filled, and was about as painful. She had hoped to feel it when she arrived in a foreign country, completely on her own—except for a few of her father's connections left over from his London tour of duty during the war; nothing. During her year in this place, she had gone out with an assortment of men who had promised to be interesting, eccentric or exciting upon first acquaintance; they had all turned out to be disappointments. Where, then, did ecstasy hide? She read James's *Varieties of Religious Experience*, underlining as she went along. The heroines in her favorite novels all met their destinies face to face: Rochester galloping out of the fog knocked Jane Eyre down. The heroes had their epiphanies—sometimes several: one for each stage along life's way. Mary Magdalene saw the risen Christ and even the working girls in ladies'-magazine fiction achieved their Great Event. When, when would she ever find the reality greater than the dream?

"There was a curious experiment done recently in America," said Dr. Empson from his armchair, his British voice deferentially easing over the consonant in such a way that she felt he was paying her a compliment. "A pair of twins were separated. Each was placed in a dark room. The light was turned on in one room. But the alpha waves of the twin in the dark responded to the light." He looked confidently about the room, sure of his effect. Members nodded to one another. As he surveyed his audience, his profile went suddenly sharp and shrewd. He was an innovator, running through an experiment. Dane thought of Mephistopheles. But then he turned and she saw his full face. His mouth curved gently, with the benevolence of an evening speaker who simply wished to share something with his listeners, something they might enjoy. Which was he? Maybe both. He wore a dark-blue polo-necked sweater. A doctor in a polo sweater. His hands were strong, expressive, with incredibly long fingers. No ring. He seemed to know much more than he was saying. She wondered what it would be like to marry such a man.

Afterward at the refreshment table, she approached him, still confident from horse breeders's whiskey. "Look," she said, touching his sleeve, then making him wait until she chewed and swallowed a ham biscuit and washed it down with sherry. "I don't know how to say this, exactly, but you have made me have some extraordinary thoughts this evening." Which was partially true. But it worked.

"Oh?" He looked down at her with real interest. "For example?"

"Oh, you make me feel that there is . . . another aristocracy in your country. An aristocracy of awareness. You're a member of it, of course—"

"Well, thank you." He smiled at her as one would at a child who has delivered a pretty compliment.

"No, no, that's not all. God, it would take all night to say what I mean."

"That's fine," he said. "I'd like to take you home. But would you mind riding on the back of a Vespa? Have you ever done that?"

"No, but I adore doing things I've never done before."

"Good girl," said Dr. Empson.

In the hotel room, Robin watched her as she unpacked his things. They were all new, bought with the ten pounds John had given Mrs. Christopher, with instructions to purchase Robin a proper holiday wardrobe. The good lady had done the word "economy" proud. Dane marveled at the quantity of child's clothes one could buy for ten pounds. She herself would have chosen differently, of course. Not so wisely, but with better taste. In future she would buy him soft expensive wools to match his pale-blue eyes (and hers), perhaps a coat with little brass buttons in the military style. She would dress him like a small cool prince and walk beside him.

He knew they were his things. He stood guard over them as she stacked the small shorts and shirts in piles. Mrs. Christopher had thought of everything: little bow ties on two shirts, a choice of red sandals or striped canvas beach shoes. Everything so small! Two bathing suits. She chose the tiny pair of yellow trunks with a green dolphin leaping up the side. The smallness of the trunks troubled and fascinated her. She held them at arm's length and pondered the marvel that they could be so little, like doll's trunks, and yet contain him.

"Come here, Robin. Let me undress you."

He yielded each stiff limb as the action was called for, not before.

"You're a little robot, that's what."

He did not answer, of course.

She took off the sailor suit, the undershirt. His faint baby smell came from his flesh to her nostrils. She took off the brown square-toed shoes (several Smarties squashed upon their soles) and his white socks. The underpants she left for last. It bothered her to see those strange puckered little genitals, so pale and not yet come to life. Perhaps if she'd had brothers, if Robin had been her own baby . . . Had she some sexual aberration about little boys? She made him stand naked before her while she looked at them and tried to decide. A shiver rippled up and down his legs, long like John's, long for his age. Something about the small naked body pulled at her. She looked down at the small perfect toes with their clipped toenails, then back at his face. Implacable. Though he was naked and chilled, his jaw thrust forward, his blue eyes were as aloof as ever. She had an unreasonable urge to do violence to him. It rose up in her throat and spilled into her mouth. What is this sweet dangerous taste? She held it still, like liquid under her tongue, trying to decipher her capacity to give or receive pain.

The feeling exploded in her, her arms flew out of their own volition, and she snatched him to her violently. She shook and rocked him and squeezed the stiff little body tight against her.

"Why won't you give in?" she said. "Why won't you love me?" She kissed the cool little face forcefully. She opened her mouth and ran her tongue quickly along the base of his neck. So clean. Then she kissed the soft brown hair smelling of baby shampoo, she kissed each of his eyes, which fluttered and closed at her touch. He neither aided nor resisted. Except for reaching up a small fist and carefully grinding from his eyes the wetness from her kisses.

"Oh, come on," she said. She grabbed the swimming trunks and hurried him into them. Then she changed into her own suit in the bathroom. He was standing by his cot when she came out, pointing to his own small suitcase beneath the cot. His face reddened and he began stamping up and down, his bare feet making little sucking noises on the floor.

"What? Can't you *say* what you want?"

He only danced and pointed; any minute he would scream.

"Hell." She crouched on the floor and went systematically through the case, holding up each item like an auctioneer. "This? This? Well, what?" When she held up a red plastic bucket and shovel Mrs. Christopher had sent along, he stopped whining and grabbed for these things.

"I'm glad we settled that." She replaced the rejects, kicked the case beneath the bed and rose wearily to her feet.

He held her hand for balance as they went downstairs. In the lobby, Ramírez-Suárez ducked playfully behind a giant potted fern, then leaped out, tweaking his moustache at Robin. The child looked at him as though he were deranged. The manager smiled sadly.

"Don't stay too long in the sun the first day, señora."

With him, she descended the stone steps leading down the steep slope onto the beach. Mother and child. She began to feel better.

45

William James said if you acted the part long enough, you became the real thing. He cluched her hand impersonally, holding tight to the red bucket and shovel with the other. Frowning, he walked first on his heels and then on his toes, curling his arches away from the steps. His small feet puckered like prawns.

The calm sea flickered, a green eye set in its sandy socket. The sunbathers lay entranced by the spell of the sun. She paused on the last step for a minute, holding him back with her. She began to unwind, gather confidence as a few people looked her way and found pleasing what they saw. Where should she spread her towel? There was a nice place near the sea, beside a rock wall.

Robin let out a piercing shriek, shattering the peace of the little beach. All the faces jerked to attention, brown and glistening with oil. He danced rapidly up and down on the stone step, reaching for her.

"What is it? What is it?" She snatched him up, but he went on screaming. Her every action formed an open-air tableau. Then he stopped shrieking and launched into great sobs. His red face was contorted against her.

An old woman in a shapeless brown bathing suit rose ponderously from a regulation army blanket, laid aside a hard-cover book and lumbered across the sand to Dane.

"Is he hurt, my dear?" she asked anxiously in a very British accent. "Has the little fellow hurt himself?

"I don't know! He started screaming just as we were standing here on the steps."

The old lady examined Robin with her liver-spotted hands. She wore a diamond on each.

"Why, it's his feet, you know. The poor little soul has burned his feet on those hot stone steps. Haven't you, darling? Where are his shoes, my dear?" She looked curiously at Dane.

"Oh God." Dane's mouth began working. She felt so exposed! She thought she would cry. "I'm a complete idiot. He had brand-new canvas beach shoes and I forgot—I forgot to put them on him." What could this woman think of her as a mother?

"Not to worry," the woman consoled her. "He's your firstborn, isn't he? I thought so, I could tell. We all make blunders with the first. It's partly because we simply don't know but also, I think, because we're trying so desperately to do everything right. The power of negative thinking, or something. I'm Mrs. Hart. Henrietta Hart. You've just arrived, haven't you?" She walked with Dane and snuffling Robin across the beach, to the vacant spot beside the wall.

"We came on today's charter from London," said Dane.

"But are you English?"

"No, American. My husband is English."

"I see," said Mrs. Hart, looking as though she would like to ask more questions, had good manners permitted. "Well, you will love Cala d'Or. It's a lovely, natural, uncomplicated spot. I've come here every summer since I lost my husband. Everyone comes back to

Cala d'Or. This is the second or third summer for most of the people here."

"Really?" Dane wanted to be agreeable. Robin squirmed to be let down. She put him down and spread her towel. "Won't you sit down, Mrs. Hart?"

"No, thank you, my dear. Once I get down, it's rather a chore to get up again. That gentleman, for instance. Do you see him sitting up there on the big rock promontory, under the shade tree, with his wife?"

Dane looked and saw a handsome Teutonic pair, middle-aged, sitting in identical striped deck chairs on their rock ledge. The man had lost his right leg at midthigh. "Yes."

"That is Mr. von Schirmbeck. He was a hero in the Afrika Korps with Rommel. He got that at Tobruk. I had two nephews and a godson killed in the last war. One might ask how I can make room in my heart for Mr. von Schirmbeck. But somehow I can. He is so nice. I wish I could speak German; I would love to have a real chat with him. Everyone who comes here is so agreeable. I think you'll find that, too." She smiled warmly at Dane, then said to Robin, who stood some feet away holding his bucket and frowning at them, "Are you feeling better, lovey?"

"He's very shy. And a little touchy today. It was his first trip in a plane."

"Oh, is that so? My grandchildren are absolutely potty about airplanes. One can't get them off, once they're on one. I'll leave you. Excuse me, I don't believe I caught your name."

"Oh, how rude of me. Dane Empson. I'm forgetting everything today."

"You were worried, dear, about your baby. Quite natural. The water is lovely and warm. I've been for a swim. You will let me know if I can be of help, Mrs. Empson, won't you? I know the island like the back of my hand—it's about the same size!—and I know the hotel and most of the guests. Also, I have raised two boys myself." Turning her mouth down at the corners, she gave Dane a friendly wink. "Cheerio for now."

"Thank you." Dane watched the old lady bearing her burden of flesh across the sand like a dignified old elephant. Such a motherly woman.

She went to the edge of the sea and put her foot in. It was warm. Robin followed tentatively, several paces behind. Mrs. Christopher had told Dane how he adored the water. The Christophers took their entire retinue of children to the Isle of Sheppey for a week every summer. Robin had to be pulled out of the water, he loved it so, she said.

"Want to go in?" Dane asked, offering him her arms. Several people on the beach watched from behind dark glasses. He didn't move. She couldn't bear to have him refuse her now. She waded determinedly into the shallow water, watching out of the corner of her eye as he fought with himself over what he wanted most: To stay separate from her, or go into the water. The water won. He moved forward with short little steps. Again she was moved by the smallness of his feet. He allowed her to lift him under the arms and pull him through the green transparency. She pulled him this way and that, improvising as she went. He smiled. Once he chuckled. But he would not look at her. He would not acknowledge her as the agent of his pleasure. The sea made him happy and he dipped his glance coyly into its depths and hummed to himself. Her arms began to ache. She saw Mr. von Schirmbeck get out of his deck chair with the aid of his crutches and swing himself expertly to the edge of the rock. He flung the crutches away, balanced for a single bright moment, his silver-gold hair catching the light, then plunged knife-sharp into the sea. He came up laughing, waved to his wife, then swirled around and swam away with clean powerful strokes, a whole man like any other in the water.

She began to cry. How magnificent that was! A pure instant of perfect courage. She turned her back on the beach people and watched the German's crisp, arrogant movement through the sea. His slashing strokes ordered her teary vision. She continued to watch and weep quietly, wondering at herself, as she pulled the boy mechanically around the warm shallows of the Mediterranean.

Chapter
Four

There was a beautiful young French couple with their two small children staying at the same hotel. Watching them was becoming Dane's secret obsession. When they were around, she could not keep her eyes from them. When they were absent, she wondered what they were doing. Everything they did seemed harmonious, of a piece. They moved in a kind of cinematic aura. Penelope had seen the Frenchwoman first. "Look at that gorgeous woman with the Paco Rabanne earrings," she told Dane and John at dinner on the night of their arrival. Dane looked, and felt a sharp pain in her chest. The woman at that moment had turned her exquisite tanned profile to her little boy in the high chair beside her. She said something in French and the child laughed delightedly. Then, across the table, the little girl laughed. The husband and wife exchanged amused looks. "Mmm. They look a nice sort of family," John commented. But Dane had taken them in and could not let them go. From

51

that moment, she measured her holiday by theirs.

Every day, Dane and Penelope lay on the beach, quickly losing their English pallor. Robin played alone in the sand, wielding his bucket and shovel into the making of large, shapeless mounds of damp sand. He made tireless trips to the edge of the water, his small shoulders bent like an old man's.

John had tried to drowse, aimless and sunstruck, with the two women. But on the morning of the third day, his daemon had prodded him from the towel, driven him, still pale, up to the balcony beneath a ponderous load of fresh ideas. He'd had Ramírez-Suárez erect a big umbrella over a table and now he sat for hours, writing on the balcony. From the beach, Dane and Penelope could look up and see the top of his head as he bent over his work.

"What's he writing?" asked Penelope.

"It's an idea he had," said Dane. "Something to do with Heraclitus and Jung's concept of enantiodromia. Overcoming your contradictions on a given level, you can swing wider, into the next level of growth. Don't ask me to explain it, because I can't." The French family were settling in directly across the beach. Their side was more in the sun. Instantly, Dane found fault with her own location.

"Is John more Jungian than Freudian?" Penelope asked. "I used to try and work it out by the books he bought when he came into the shop. But I gave up, because they were mostly philosophy and science fiction. When I got up the nerve to talk to him, he said 'eclectic.' That means a little of everybody, I believe. Since I've been going to him, it occurs to me he's not terribly Freudian because he hasn't asked me much about my childhood. He's mostly interested in what I'm thinking and feeling now."

"Maybe he's starting with your outermost layer and working in," Dane suggested, imagining John plucking Penelope's psyche like an artichoke. She shrugged and buried her head between her arms and pretended to be hard at sunbathing. When people started asking what John "was," she became tense and defensive. She didn't know herself. Sometimes she felt she'd been deceived, but if so it was by her own false assumptions. John had never pretended to be anything but his strange nebulous self.

("But you *are* a qualified doctor?"

"I am. Go down to my office. You'll find a BMA register. I'm there, under the E's. So is Somerset Maugham, who never practiced a day in his life."

"But you're not a *psychiatrist.*"

"I never said I was one."

"Well, what are you?"

"I'm a psychotherapist. But that's not going to make you feel better, because any quack in England can hang out a shingle with 'Psychotherapist' on it. This isn't your regulated America, where everything is licensed."

"Are you saying you are a quack, then?"

"I'm saying I can't be neatly labeled, as you've been trying to do ever since we married and you started going through my bank statements and nagging me about the world. I happen to know I can help people. I have some answers."

"Well, think how many more people you might help—would come to you—if you had your DPM. You could get it from the Maudsley in two years and call yoursef a psychiatrist."

"I have enough patients. The ones who interest me don't come because of my credentials. Why waste two years reading a lot of boring textbooks? I'm beyond them. I'm onto *real* things with energy in them. I can't wait for 'the world' to catch up. By then I'd be dead. People will be studying *my* textbooks at the Maudsley when I'm dead. Only, by then, there'll be a new chap, like me, who's gone beyond and can't be bothered with my boring textbooks."

Well, what should I tell my father you are?"

"Tell him anything that will make you happy. I've been a math scholar, philosopher, computer programmer, doctor who delivers babies—that was fun, very *joyful*—and, of course, I was almost a Jesuit. I've been all those things and I'm none of them now. Next year I may be something else again. I'm evolving all the time. I'm not your 'finished' man, I'm afraid. To be finished is to be circumscribed, to have stopped growing. Then one might as well be dead."

"It's only—well, I wish you wanted to be a little more *respectable*."

"I am respectable. I'm probably the most

respectable person you'll ever meet. You mean conventional. That's what you mean.")

"John is exceptional," Dane mumbled to Penelope from her towel. "You can't fit him into any category. Some of him always evades it. One day he will probably make some terrible breakthrough and his name will be famous."

"Oh, John is brilliant," the girl agreed. "Whenever he talks to me, I get these glimmers of things. Things beyond where *my* mind can go."

Dane felt better. She studied her French family. The man and woman lay side by side on a towel, profiles to the sun. They had the dignified calm of royal Egyptian mummies. Their children played healthily by the sea.

Both the man and the woman were very tall and elongated, like El Greco figures. They had been here for a month almost, according to Mrs. Hart. She would have found out more, only the old lady spoke no French. Both of them were a deep cocoa brown. He was lean and angular with jet-black hair and a sexy smile which he saved for his wife alone. He moved swiftly, stealthily across the beach, like a native in his jungle. The woman was lean and pointed, too, in face, neck and limbs. But her body was womanly, snapped back into shape after childbearing, healthy and ready to bear more. She wore an extremely brief white bikini which would have looked repulsive on most women. But it became part of her nakedness rather than setting it off. When she walked, toes curling into the sand, she thrust her pelvis forward, and the round tightness of her belly glistened with oil. It was possible that she might even be carrying a tiny baby inside her now; she bore herself with a drowsing, secretive quality. The childen, a boy and a girl, were called Manuel and Valerie. She often called to them in her musical voice. They went without tops and had identical haircuts and were plump and very brown.

The mother took one or sometimes both of them into the sea. Or the four of them went together. They splashed and laughed and found one another so endlessly amusing that soon everyone on the beach was watching them hungrily. Sometimes the Frenchman and his wife went alone. He would duck suddenly beneath the water and she would leap up screaming like a schoolgirl. Once Dane watched her climb on his shoulders and stand poised on long glistening brown legs. Then she dived from his body into the clear green sea.

Sometimes she left them and went to swim by herself, musing and dreaming, her black hair swept back like some water sprite's. In her own good time, she would return to them, padding sleepily up the beach, wringing her hair with her hands and rocking a little on her heels, and go down gracefully beside the man on the towel.

Penelope said, "I suppose the two of you have these fascinating conversations late at night. I always imagine Beethoven playing in the background."

"Sometimes Beethoven," said Dane. She remembered a night several weeks ago. He had hovered behind her chair, passing back and forth on mysterious errands as she tried to read. Suddenly she snatched up a pencil and underlined a passage. He stopped to look over her shoulder.

"Interesting," he said. "Why did you underline it?"

She had thrown the book at him, an old copy of *The Cloud of Unknowing* she'd found that afternoon while browsing among Watkins' Booksellers' dusty mystical tracts. "Can't I have anything of my own!" she had cried, going to the whiskey cabinet and pouring herself a full glass of cognac. He disapproved of drinking because it lowered awareness. She gulped it down, picked up *Cloud* and went off to the guest room. He followed. After a token knock on the slammed door, he entered, looking befuddled and malevolent at the same time.

"I only thought we might reach a shared moment of truth," he said. The light hit his glasses, turning him metallic-blind.

"I'm going to sleep in here. I've got to have some space to myself," she said.

"I see. Well, call me if you need me. Good night, my dear."

After he left, she drank more cognac. She stewed and felt abused. Then she heard him going out. The front door closed. The Vespa was gunned, then roared away. He was going to that dingy all-night café in Charing Cross to play chess with an old dope addict, the only person in town who could give John a good game. The man had once been a well-known barrister. She could see the two of them hunched over the game in that smoky place. The old man played intuitively, like a bright child, John had told her. She started back into the living room to get some more cognac, but the dark hall was crammed with shadows and shapes of her own making. John had left her to fend them off alone. She hurried back to the guest room and locked the door. She wrote a poem, which she planned to slip under John's door after he came back, and went to sleep:

> *Heaven is not Noah's Ark—*
> *Each must founder in his dark.*
> *I may get there; so may you;*
> *But not like the animals, two by two.*

She needed to go to the bathroom, but couldn't face that hallway. Feeling thoroughly isolated from reality, she squatted over a flowerpot and urinated in that. She supposed the plant would die. She lay on top of the bed, still wearing her clothes, and waited for him to come back to free her from that room. But he stayed gone till dawn, came back refreshed and alert, knocked on her door and offered to take her to breakfast somewhere. Exhausted, punished, she accepted gratefully. She never gave him the poem, because the moment was past.

"I wish I were madly in love," said Penelope.

"Maybe you will be soon," Dane replied.

"You can imagine what it's like when they have intercourse," Penelope sighed.

"Who?"

"That French couple that you're always looking at. How nice, if one could fit together with someone else, as they obviously do, and have Beethoven as well."

Dane did not like the implications of this remark, and said, "Oh, they no doubt have their problems. He's probably a clerk in a bank and they fight over money all the time."

"I suppose," Penelope agreed. But she continued to look across the beach.

Not wishing to share her beautiful family with Penelope, Dane opened John's copy of Yeats and bowed deeply over it. She had been bringing it down to the beach each day, hoping to find in its underlined passages why she and John were unhappy together. But the underscored lines seemed totally unrelated to the man she knew. She found other passages, not marked, which suited him far more. Why, for instance: "And paced among the mountains overhead/And hid his face amid a crowd of stars"? Why not instead: "The fascination of what's difficult/Has dried the sap out of my veins, and rent/Spontaneous joy and natural content/Out of my heart"?

Of course, it was sixteen years ago. Could he have changed so much, or was she failing to see what was there all along? She often tried to picture John at nineteen, a student in the flush of youth. But this picture always eluded her. There was something ageless about him, like a magician. Other times, he seemed like a very old man. And sometimes, the times she couldn't bear him, he was like a baby.

John had told her about a spring day at

Oxford, when he was nineteen, that changed his life. There he was, God-promised, about to take his first vows as a Jesuit. He'd been sitting in the Bodleian, plowing through the *Summa*, when suddenly he heard a bicycle bell and he looked outside the window and saw a young girl with a yellow flower in her hair riding her bicycle in the sun. "I saw that I was about to renounce things I'd never really experienced, retiring into God, unlived." Perhaps, at this time, he had gone about underlining the star passages in poems.

"Such a solemn little poppet, Robin," said Penelope. "Packing away at that lump of sand as though he were doing something very urgent indeed. Does he ever talk?"

"Sometimes," Dane said.

So far Robin had wet his bed every night and sometimes during his afternoon nap. No matter how often Dane put him on the pot, he seemed to summon up more. She could not face the two maids who cleaned the room. One morning she was on the balcony when they came. She heard them shaking the covers of the little cot and her smattering of Spanish was sufficient to cause her shame. "*Pobrecito*," they murmured. "*Sí, sí, qué lástima*," they mourned, changing the sheets.

She looked at him now, the pale little back turned aloofly away, and she wanted to touch him. "Come over here, Robin, let me rub some cream on you again." He liked to have the cool stuff rubbed on him, so he came at once, frowning and clutching the red bucket. She anchored him between her knees and took her time rubbing his soft tummy with the cream. The pliancy of his baby flesh against the pressure of her fingertips fascinated her. She pressed too hard and he gave a sharp little grunt.

"Sorry. Turn around and let me do the back of you."

She spun him like a zombi and began massaging the cream into the nape of his neck and working it down, in slow sensuous strokes, toward the small of his back, where the little buttocks began their rise at the line of his swimming trunks. When she finished, she held him by his upper arms and swayed him back and forth, the rigid little doll. She put her face against his neck and smelled him. Then, as he wriggled to get away, she planted quick compulsive kisses over the entire surface of his back. She abstained from a wild desire to sink her teeth into him.

"Did I ever tell you about the day I went to pieces in Fortnum's?" Penelope said.

"No, but I'd be interested to hear," said Dane. He was struggling now; she had to let him go. Back he went, taking his soft flesh with him, to the amophous sand mound.

"It was in jams and jellies," Penelope began, perking up. She was already a lovely golden pink. He hair had lightened from light brown to afternoon gold and she wore it in a single braid started high on her head. It gave her the air of an archaic courtly maiden. "I had gone there during my lunch hour to buy a jar of Oxford marmalade. The man was ever so nice. You know how they bow to you, all dressed up in their morning coats. Then I thought of my mother's breakfast table, and all of us sitting round on a Sunday morning, my brothers and their wives when it's a holiday. And I thought: *They* have a right to Oxford marmalade, but do I? What difference does it make? Sainsbury's would do just as well for Miss Penelope, all alone in her fancy dressing gown which nobody's going to see, sitting in her two-by-four bed-sitter on Sundays and wolfing down her very own breakfast while reading wistfully about Tony and Margaret in the *Times.* I felt so depressed, I suddenly felt—it was as if I had seen into the future—that nothing important would ever happen to me. I could go for years, buying jams and dressing gowns for nobody to enjoy but me. I burst into tears, right there in Fortnum's. The man was so kind. He asked would I like to sit down. I told him I often got these excruciating backaches, they simply came on without warning. But I could never go back there again."

"But why shouldn't you have Oxford marmalade, if you like it?" Dane said. "I mean, those are wonderful days, when one is free and uncommitted and everything is possible. I look back with real nostalgia on those days. Before I met John, I had just taken this lovely flat overlooking the houseboats on the Thames. I remember how I could spin out an entire Sunday by myself: Bloody Marys for breakfast, then the book review sections of the *Times* and the *Observer*, then I'd look up the movies and decide which one I should go to in the afternoon. You should treasure your Oxford-marmalade days."

"Yes, you can afford to say things like that," said Penelope, "because you have the other now. You can afford to look back and be nostalgic because you're no longer trapped in that sort of life."

"Every life has its little traps," said Dane, and didn't intend to say a sentence more. She sighed and turned on her towel, balancing herself on one elbow so she could flip through Yeats and spy on the French family as well. The woman sat up to rub oil on her legs and looked across the beach toward Dane. Suddenly the gazes of the two women fused. Dane was the first to look away. She read her husband's underlines: "The horse that comes from the road,/The rider, the birds that range/From cloud to tumbling cloud,/Minute by minute they change . . ." Yet, only four lines above, she found what she would have picked for John to mark as his: "Hearts with one purpose alone /Through summer and winter seem/Enchanted to a stone . . ."

Had I come across this book, underlined as it is, with a stranger's name instead of John Dominick Empson, Merton College, penned on the flyleaf, I would have fallen in love with that stranger, she thought. Hoping to catch the stranger unaware, she looked up quickly at John, writing on his balcony. The white wall around it blocked off all but his head, shaded by the big umbrella. But the stranger was not there. She was glad that the wall hid his body. She liked his head best anyway. The rest of him gave her problems. His flesh-and-blood failings which he dumped regularly in her lap like so much bruised fruit made it more and more difficult for her to keep the image clean. He could not balance her on his shoulders in the sea, or stride silently as a native across a sandy beach. His daily dealings with life were so much smaller than the panoramic sweep of his mind; his actions were never quite worthy of the clean, heroic beauty of his best ideas.

"I think I'll go for a swim," said Penelope.

Chapter
Five

There were several moments before dinner each evening when Dane felt she was partly on show and partly on trial. She dressed for these moments and tried to compose herself for the time when she and John, and Robin between them, descended the stairs, and the guest already assembled outside the dining-room doors would turn to look. Mr. von Schirmbeck, leaning on his crutches, might be reading aloud to his rosy-cheeked wife the evening menu, which Ramírez-Suárez typed and posted on the doors. Mrs. Hart would be chatting with whoever was available. Ramírez-Suárez would stride importantly about, looking at his wristwatch so he could open the door on the dot of seven. The French family usually gathered near the front door, and every evening the woman wore an outfit more stunning than that of the evening before.

When the stern dark English doctor with his blue-eyed wife and son came down, everyone looked at them. The von Schirmbecks looked politely interested, Ramírez-Suárez went cheerful at the sight of the child, and Mrs. Hart came to claim them in conversation. The French family were the most cursory in their glances toward the descending Empsons. Dane would have loved to catch one gram of interest or envy in the Frenchwoman's brief gaze. But it was not to be, apparently.

"I don't think her husband could be a bank clerk," Penelope said at dinner. "Did you see the cut of that green linen pants suit?"

"Well, perhaps they're royalty in disguise, or billionaires, and have their yacht hidden just beyond the cove," said Dane dryly. "Perhaps they're only here to slum." She sloshed more wine in her glass. Her head ached slightly. Why would John never notice when people needed more wine? They'd decided to make an outing to Pedro's Bar after dinner. It was the only social outlet in Cala d'Or. The hotel guests walked into the village in the evening, browsed in the souvenir shops, then crossed over to Pedro's to sit at the round tables and drink and stare at one another. There was to be a little dance band up from Palma tonight and Penelope was eager to go, positive a dance partner would materialize.

Now Dane said, "I think I'll stay here tonight. I'll stay with Robin."

"But—" Penelope began. Poor thing, she was afraid they would spoil her chances.

"Robin's all right by himself," John said. "Ramírez-Suárez loves to check on him by the half hour."

"I didn't mean that. It's just that I have a bit of a headache. But I want you two to go on, as planned. If you say no, then I'll insist on going, headache or no headache." She laughed sharply. "I'll make everyone feel guilty."

John agreed to go with Penelope. "When did this headache begin?" he asked, watching her closely.

"It's just the sun," she said. "I'll be good as new when you get back tonight." She could afford to be generous, up to a point, now that she'd won the evening for herself.

As soon as dinner was over, she lifted Robin down from his chair and led him away. She looked forward to the stairs, tugging him up each one, he slightly pulling back.

Alone in the room with him, she knelt before him and unbuttoned his shirt. She folded each little garment and stacked it in a pile. She made him wait naked, while she deposited the things to be washed in a corner of the closet, put the rest in a drawer and returned with his pajamas. She led him to the bathroom, knelt again and sponged experimentally at his face. Once she had seen Mrs. Christopher swipe it as casually as you would a windshield. She placed him on the toilet seat and watched how he gripped hard with his hands on either side, to keep his balance. So perfectly helpless he was, braced for dear life on that rim. What if she should walk out on him now, leave him tottering there? She wondered what he'd do. Then she helped him into his pajamas and carried him to bed, holding him close against her and smelling his hair.

When she had tucked him in, she leaned over close to his face and said, "Well, are you going to say good night tonight?"

His impassive look hurled all her frustrations back at her.

"I've heard you talk," she went on. "I know you could say it any time you wanted. I'll bet you say it to Mrs. Christopher. Oh, forget it." She had to turn away from him then, she had such a longing to slap some expression into the cool impervious little face.

She moved about, tidying up. She had always been neat—her military father had seen to that—but lately she was becoming obsessive about order. An object out of place, a pair of shoes unaligned, had the power to send her into a vile mood these days. John had left a messy pile of foolscap notes on a corner of the dresser. She straightened the edges and several lines of scrawl at the bottom of a page caught her eye:

The beginning of this process is often characterized by a person's getting stuck in a blind alley: a so-called impossible situation. What happens next is extremely ...

Eagerly, she turned to the next page, but it was blank. She went without shame to John's suitcase and rifled through stacks of notes he'd made on previous days. She was searching for something she'd often found before: notes about herself, him, their marriage. Back in

London, she hurried to the bottom drawer of his desk every time he went out. She usually found a new analysis of herself, or an interesting comment on the progress of their marriage. It was intriguing, to read about herself in suspenseful installments. What would "D" do next? (That was how he referred to her in his jottings.) And he was such a faithful and acute observer. She was learning all sorts of things about herself.

D has an extraordinarily wide play of mind, but she is also a masochist.

Once she had read that. A masochist, was she? She tested this new insight. Mmm. Perhaps she was, a bit. His having ascribed the label to her, she took a sort of pride in it. After all, she must be special, for him to chart her daily, as if she were some rare bird of infinite fascination.

Sometimes he quoted. Oddly enough, her sayings that he so proudly transcribed had often been flung at him during their fights; they had been epithets coined in opposition to him and what he wanted of her:

"How sick I am of people giving plaid stamps with their neuroses!"

—D

"As I see it, all 'mothering' is debilitating to the real man. When you 'mother' someone, what you're really doing is anticipating his failure."

—D last night

He made allowances for her toward the improvement of their marriage:

With D I have learned that one must accept an imperfect equal's imperfections for the sake of mutual growth. Else abandon the idea of intimacy in marriage altogether and retreat instead into impractical dreams of perfect partners—as D does, even now.

Sometimes he felt sorry for himself:

Went for a walk at dawn by the Embankment. D never goes along now, sleeps till noon. Sky just lightening . . . birds . . . barges steaming downriver. Thought of V, how she always waked with me, walked with me, how she *felt* the morning. Missed her and her bountiful love . . .

But always backed her up, in the end:

. . . but V could never have made it, where I've got to. Better this tension with D, who remains the only potential companion for my safaris. Tension leads to growth.

She had particularly liked:

D resists being pulled below the line. Her defenses are ultimately retentive ones: retention of *Dane* against all efforts to undermine her *Danishness*.

It was as if she'd been assigned her colors: Orioles from Baltimore were black and orange; Danes were difficult.

But tonight she found slim pickings:

Places undercut human beings. Anna Karenina and Vronsky fall to pieces in absence of former milieu. Enduring relationships demand the framework of a place, can only be as real as the place is mutual to the two parties. Holiday relationships are an exception, can be suspended in a sort of void outside the frameworks of both parties because of the limited *time*.

What was that supposed to mean? Was that all? Not one word about D. Or R. Or even P.

Sighing through her teeth, she put the papers back in his suitcase and went out on the balcony. One last mauve remnant of sky pushed back the night. A single star, or planet, shone above the tiny island and its ruined fort. The sea lapped amiably and the air was cool, perfect for sunburned lovers. She sat down. On the terrace, directly two floors below, some Germans played a warlike game of Ping-Pong. Deadly serious. Toc-toc . . . toc-toc . . . "Ach! *Verdamnt!* . . ." A paddle slammed against a table. Guttural consonants rose like heat to her ears. Then one of them laughed. The game resumed.

That Vespa ride, on the evening of their meeting, had been the nearest she'd got to her Peak Experience. There was one pellucid moment—she could still go back and recapture it. They had been careening just toward the first lion at the bottom of Trafalgar Square; she held tightly to the rough knit around his waist, a little frightened of the speed but loving its thrill. And she looked between the space where the wind had separated his hair into two blue-black wings and pressed her full face at the cold sky and felt she was at last aboard some terrible and wonderful machine driven by a dark angel who would take her, whether she balked or not, to her destiny. I made him ask me, she thought. They shot under the Admiralty Arch and roared down the deserted pink-cobbled Mall, straight toward where the flag announced the Queen was sleeping, and Dane, who now felt she could do anything, laid her cheek flat against this strange man's broad back, and at once his elbows closed down upon her arms in response. Possibly that was to be the best moment she would ever have with him.

At that time, Dane had just won an increase in salary and had moved to a spacious one-room flat on the upper floor of an old Cheyne Walk house. It was the sort of place she had always wanted: a large room, all her own, with upholstered window seats in the bay windows and a view to look at which would change from minute to minute. Now she had it. Her windows faced the bend in the river just below Albert Bridge where a dozen or so highly individualized houseboats clustered. At night, she loved to pull the heavy velvet curtains and then climb in beneath them, onto her window seat, and be able to watch the people in the houseboats and the boats going up and downriver, without their seeing her. The bay windows jutted out from the house, making it seem that she was floating through the black sky, watching the world from her warm, carpeted bubble, which also had a little kitchen (where she kept books on the shelves meant for cans) and even an American-style bathroom.

She had just moved in the week before and he was the first man to enter here. She was interested in his reactions to the luxurious gray-green carpet, the abundance of comfortable chairs and polished tables, the antique writing desk with pigeonholes, the framed hunting prints on the ivory-colored walls. It was not the sort of place many young single working girls usually lived in. But he went in, pleasantly enough, sat down in one of the comfortable chairs she offered, declined a whiskey, and made no comment at all on her lovely room. He didn't seem to notice it. She decided his own place must be a hundred times superior and he refrained from commenting on her modest quarters out of politeness.

"Won't you at least drink some coffee?" she urged. The Trafalgar Square mood was slipping away. She had trapped this rare creature and got him to her flat and now she had no idea what to do with him.

"If it's no trouble, I'd like some," he said. *He* seemed perfectly at his ease. She hurried to the little kitchen to put on some water. Just as she was filling the kettle, he appeared in the doorway. "What I like about you is, you haven't closed down," he said, out of the blue. "Most people, by the time they're twenty or so, have hardened into what they'll remain for the rest of their lives. But somehow it's missed you. You haven't given up."

"What makes you say that?" She was amazed. She turned to face him. They were very close in the little kitchen. "How can you tell that?" She wasn't sure what he meant, even.

He laughed. "It was easy. Seeing things like . . . what I saw in you is my business. Oh, you're a soul on the prowl, all right." But he was looking at her with a sort of amused affection. Her social flutterings were calmed.

She began to ask him questions, things she really cared about. They sat side by side in her window seat, above the dark river. Lights hung from the cables of the bridge; they glittered as the bridge swayed in the night wind. "Have you ever had a vision?" she asked. "Has there ever been a perfect illuminated moment in your life when you knew the universe was speaking personally, just to you?"

He laughed. "I have them every day."

"Oh, you're making fun of me."

"No. I'm serious. Visions have been there, will be there, for all times. What we're lacking in our time are men who can see. You can have them. It's simply a matter of recognizing what is already there."

"Could you help me to . . . recognize?"

He thought about this. "Perhaps I could," he said, pondering her with the great brown eyes. He didn't seem to see a girl, rather attractive, long-limbed, blue-eyed, with the latest fashion in shoes and a suit cut in Paris. He saw, she believed—what was it he had said?—"a soul on the prowl." He seemed to look straight into the vast secret core of her that contained all her best possibilities.

"You make everything—but what matters —seem so phony!" she cried. "You just bore into it with those X-ray eyes and show it for what it is. *I'm* a phony, in a lot of ways."

"You weren't phony when you approached me," he said. "You knew what you wanted to say, you came up and said it. I liked that. All you need is to sort out what you're for and what you're against. Then live by that. You seem to do it now, more than most." And he smiled at her again, approvingly.

After he'd gone, she remembered how she hadn't liked his teeth when he smiled. They were dusky and grew inward, like so many Britishers'; they were her first disappointment about him. But then a week passed and there was no word from him and first her pride was hurt and she focused on the teeth to assuage it. After that she began idealizing him, and the teeth, the slight limp she had noticed when he crossed her room, anything she could remember became a touchpoint over which she could linger nostalgically: the way he had of cradling his coffee cup, as though he needed to warm his hands; those airy gestures he made with his fingers, which seemed to accompany some inner vision. She pictured him dressed in a suit, sitting behind a large impressive desk, his hands folded attentively as he listened to a patient. And the picture hurt her—in the same way it used to tear her heart out to watch her boyfriends play in a football game—because there was this man, involved in something which had nothing to do with her. To torture herself, she looked up his name in the directory. He lived within fifteen minutes' walking distance! She imagined herself dialing his number, saying coyly, "Remember me?" and interrupting him at just the wrong time, and him saying, "I wonder, could I ring you back later? I'm in the midst of something rather urgent," and she cringed with humiliation, as though this had really happened. She imagined herself walking to his street, just to look at his house, and bumping into him coming out of it with another woman. "Um, were you coming to see me?" he would ask politely, and the woman on his arm would smile aloofly, waiting for him to get done with this bothersome girl.

Another week passed. She began to lose the reality of him, of the evening altogether. She vacillated between thinking: He was too special, so of course he wouldn't have wanted me, and: What was so special about him, anyway? She gave a buffet dinner at her new place and invited some people from the magazine and a couple of young attachés from the American Embassy, who were square but who always brought her good whiskey from the PX. Back in the flurry of her schedule, she saw the rather cold oddity of him. An older couple, friends of her father, invited her for a weekend at their country house. She sat around the garden, commenting on their daffodils and drinking gin and tonics and entertaining them with highly exaggerated anecdotes about the odd birds she met during the course of her job.

"There was this mad doctor lecturing on ESP to the Mensas; he insisted on taking me home on the back of his scooter and told me he had a vision every day and, what was more, he could make me have them, too," she heard herself say gaily, and wondered why lightning didn't strike her.

"Better watch *that* sort," her host had cautioned, going on to talk of his own niece, how she'd been slipped LSD in a drink at a party. He was a military man, a career officer like her father, a little stodgy, but comforting. For all Dane knew, Dr. Empson might be a hophead.

On the following Saturday came his letter. It was written in black ink on gray paper in an irregular schoolboyish scrawl. It said, simply:

I've thought about this since I left you. I am quite sure, now. All the potential is there for us to create a shared universe greater than either of us could make (or explore) alone. I never had this certainty with anyone before.

It was signed John Empson, and that was all.

She went over and over those four sentences, her heart beating uncomfortably. So he hadn't forgotten her. Far from it, it seemed. But what was this formidable announcement? Was he asking her to marry him? He hadn't even addressed her by name in the letter. No "Dear . . ."; not even a date. The postmaster said the letter had been mailed at 3 P.M. the day before. Maybe not marriage. Maybe this was his curious way to offer her a platonic friendship. They could go on field trips together in search of visions. Never had that certainty with anyone before, had he? What had she said to impress him so? She went back over their conversation. She *had* given him a rather agreeable fashion show of the many facets of her mind. He was probably attracted to her sexually as well, only didn't want to admit it. She imagined him making love to her. Except for those earnest brown eyes, it came across in the style of Bluebeard. She shivered with thrill and recoil, went and poured herself a drink, and walked up and down her big carpeted room. The gray sheet of paper fluttered in her hand like a bleak bird restless to return with her answer. What answer? The letter hadn't asked for one. If anything, it assumed the existence of an answer before the question was asked. God, it almost seemed as if *she* had asked the question and he had thought about it for three weeks and sent an answer. Damn him, how dare he assume! A dozen games clicked into her mind which could shatter him with uncertainty and make him reassess his facile assurance. If she let three weeks pass, say, then sent him a light little note, inviting him to tea, and invited some others to come as well! He would wonder: Does she want me? Did she want him? She wanted to be given the choice of wanting or not wanting him, to be handed in toto the bundle of his quirks and qualities and go leisurely through, sorting and sifting and deciding for herself while he waited for her verdict. But this: it was a bid to a secret, exclusive society to which you couldn't ask to know the special handshake, the private rituals before joining. He had put it on another level, where she didn't know her footing. She couldn't stand the possibility that she might forfeit perhaps her greatest opportunity by playing inferior games. She went out, got a taxi and gave his address, which of course she knew by heart. No longer in doubt of being welcomed, she would simply go and see what he had in mind. Nobody could make her do anything.

His house was situated on a cheerful square, very much as she'd imagined it from the outside. It was a row house on a well-kept street in a fashionable part of town; exactly what a young doctor should have. She used the brass knocker, which could have used some polish. When no one responded, she rang the bell. Presently she heard steps muffled by carpet. The door heaved once, twice. A man, unshaven, stood before her in a woolen bathrobe. He squinted into the bright light.

"Oh, it *is* you!" she said, finally recognizing him. "You looked different without your glasses." But she felt wrong; he looked startled. She could see past him into the hall of the house. It was a brownish dark.

"Yes, I see," he said then. "You must have got my letter." His eyes were velvety soft, slightly unfocused without the glasses. He seemed to be trying hard to get himself together.

"Why don't I come back, when you're more awake?" she said, a bit irritated at the awkwardness of the situation.

"No, please. I've been awake. I've been sitting around playing chess by myself. Please come in. I had rather hoped you might ring up or come round." Now he looked as if he were afraid she'd go away.

"If you're sure . . ." She went ahead of him into the dark hall.

"Upstairs. The part down here is for patients." He indicated she should go up some carpeted stairs into an even gloomier part of the house.

The hall above had massive walnut bookcases on either side. The books didn't seem to be in any particular order. She saw medical books, novels, psychology, science fiction paperbacks, all mingled.

"In here," he said, opening a door and going ahead of her into a room where everything seemed to be shades of brown. All the furniture looked like the sort which had once belonged in much bigger rooms—except for a garish lime-green sofa, which was newer than anything in the room and made of some synthetic material. There was one enormous canvas hanging over a buffet. It was an abstract, done all in blacks and whites, rather sinister. It did nothing to warm the room. Dane took all this in instantly and was heavily disappointed. If this were *her* house, she would call the Salvation Army and say, "Come pick up all this furniture," then she would have men come and scrub the place from top to bottom and paint all the walls white. After that, she'd begin again. This room, for instance, looked out on a cheerful square, where beds of red tulips shimmered in the late May sunshine. Why not have curtains the color of the tulips? They would look perfect against the freshly painted white walls—

"Won't you sit down?" he said, calling her back to the room with yellow walls and dark-green curtains.

She sat down on the garish sofa, because it looked the most uncluttered place. There was a unique-looking chess set laid out beneath her on the floral carpet.

"What a lovely set!" she cried.

"Yes," he agreed. "I was just having a game when you arrived."

"With yourself! How can you play with yourself?"

"Easy. Pretend to be two people." He stood looking down at her calmly while she bent to finger the pieces, each of which was individually carved. In fact, it was not really a set at all. She couldn't understand how he played with them. Every piece was the same color. All the faces were rosy, flesh-toned, like little people. Where was the distinction between sides?

"I'll get you some coffee," he offered.

"No, don't bother—"

"I was about to have some myself. It's made."

"Well, okay, I would like it, then."

He all but bolted from the room in the old woolen bathrobe. He came back dressed in a pair of old trousers and the same navy sweater, coffee sloshing from a mug held in each hand, his glasses on, his pale face bearing signs of a hasty shave. He sat down beside her on the sofa. "My letter made sense to you, then."

"It was a challenge," she said cautiously.

"You're a girl who likes challenges," he replied easily.

"I never thought I'd see you again," she said, veering off.

"Didn't you really?"

"No. People like you happen only in novels."

"I see." He looked pleased. "How do you account for me *now*, then?"

"I'm not sure. But you make me want to read on."

"That's everything with a person like you," he said, smiling.

"I love your chess set," she repeated.

"I do, too. A former patient of mine carved it. A young Yugoslav. We used to play. It's not an ordinary set, you see. It's a set consisting entirely of his own myths. He saw these myths as negative or positive, in terms of his own life. The interesting part was this: he never told me which piece was negative and which was positive. I, as the person who knew him best, had to guess which piece was which to him. If I failed, I was penalized at the beginning of the game by forfeiting the piece, since it was never mine in the first place."

"Wait, I don't understand," said Dane, becoming excited.

"Look: at the beginning of a chess game, each person sets up his pieces, right?"

"Right."

"Good. So say I decide to take the positive pieces. I'm pretty confident in reaching for his black-hooded queen with the snake coiled round her waist, because as his therapist I have come to know what that queen represents. And although a mysterious, sinister figure to some, this queen I know to be generative for him, therefore positive. So far, so good? Then, however, say I take *this* piece, the Green Knight—you know him?—for positive because I myself associate it with positive connotations: fertility, rebirth, so on. Well, when I did do this, I lost the Green Knight because it happened to be a negative myth for Pavel. He took it over to his side and removed the knight I *should* have chosen: this white crusader with his red cross. I was without one of my knights at the start of the game. Yet, a week later, these knights had reversed their roles in his life, and I ended up losing my knight again!"

"But that's so nebulous," protested Dane. "How can you play a game where the rules keep changing?"

"That's the most interesting kind," he said. "I'm sorry Pavel died. I've found no one since with such an exciting mind. I go on playing with his set, imagining he's sitting across the board, but it's not the same. I often beat this Pavel; the living one was always changing, one step ahead of me."

"But how did he die?"

"Shot himself one morning."

"But why?" She was incensed. Shouldn't the doctor *save* his patient?"

"He had this theory about a time shield. He believed if one could manage to get behind it, one could join the world of spirit with the world of matter. That may sound deluded to you. But, in his own terms, I think he killed himself in a moment of profound joy."

"God." She shivered, close to tears. "Just hearing about him makes him seem so real—almost as if I knew him. I can just see him: a thin, proud young man. Blond. His clothes don't fit properly. Very big eyes, rather haunted. He's holding himself in, squeezing tighter and tighter until he feels he's going to burst any moment. He squeezes behind this illusory golden shield and at that moment he *does* burst —bang!—into a million pieces which float off into the air like motes in a sunbeam. I can see it, I honestly can." This room, this strange talk, were having their effects on her. She did have a perfect picture of poor Pavel, as if he stood there before her.

"Of course you can," said John proudly. "That's because you haven't closed down. I saw this in you the other night. I want you permanently in my life. And you. How about you? Do you want it, too?"

"I think I do," she said. Her face felt numb. His compelling words held her in a sort of reckless bondage of her own making. She looked into his eyes and he looked back with such solemnness that she felt the beginnings of vertigo. She thought she might throw up or faint if she didn't get out of this house.

"Why don't we go for a walk?" she said. "It's such a nice day."

They walked along the Embankment and crossed the bridge into Battersea Park. It was crammed with healthy families, having their Saturday outing. John's face took on color, he walked beside her smiling to himself and made small talk about the flowers and the animals in the little zoo. Dane began to feel better. And she had got him back, after all!

They stopped in front of a parrot cage. "Robin loves these parrots," he said.

"Who is Robin?"

"My son. He's two. He's illegitimate."

"Oh? What's he like?" She was not going to show the least bit of surprise.

John smiled to himself and went on watching the parrots. "Quite extraordinary, in his own little way. I like to think he's like me as a child. I want you to meet him. He boards at a foster home at the moment. According to law, I can adopt him when I marry. Oh, he's a species all by himself," and he chuckled quietly. "You are just the person who should be his mother."

She said nothing. Again, there was the funny numbness in her face. He took her silence as acquiescence. He knew what he wanted and assumed she did, too.

They recrossed the bridge. He stopped midway, at its highest point, and leaned over the railing, deep in thought. The wind separated his hair into the two blue-black wings and she wondered what he saw. Then, almost absently, he took her left hand in his, perused the fingers. A police boat purred efficiently through the nickel-colored Thames beneath.

"I shall have to get you a nice ring," he said. "I think we should have it made, something entirely your own."

And she said nothing. It was as eloquent and decisive as leaping over the bridge. She forced herself to look at him, rebounding a bit from that terrible brown intensity. All she wished for now was to complete her self-abnegation to the will of this determined man.

"I think I want to go to bed with you— this afternoon," she mumbled through frozen lips.

"Darling," he said, holding her in the terrible gaze.

They went back to his dark house. He led her to his bedroom, filled with more brown furniture. The bedclothes were in a turmoil and there was a faint smell of unwashed socks about the place. As they undressed, he wouldn't let her look away from him. Repelled by the room, by his intensity, she nevertheless felt a perverse and heady passion rising in her body. She had often wondered how martyrs felt, the moment before they were devoured by fire, or nuns, when their hair is being cut off, just before taking the veil. It must be something like this. He took her rather quickly, but it didn't matter. She lay there afterward feeling totally obliterated by his will. She felt she had, at last, done something irrevocable.

Toc-toc . . . toc-toc . . . *"Der sieger!"* Silence, and a goat ninnied from a farm. Dane stood up and went to the balcony wall. She hung over it, spying on the people below. There were little colored lights strung round the terrace and they lit the faces of the drinkers. There was the beautiful French couple, sipping their Pernods, leaning toward each other across the table. He was telling her something, some anecdote. She pressed her glass sensually with the tips of her fingers and looked into its depths, listening and smiling slightly. Her sleek black hair swung forward, cupping her fine profile. She made Dane's heart ache, she was so perfect. She went on watching them avidly. It was dark and they couldn't see her, but she could see every expression on their faces, she could enter into their space without them ever knowing.

Then the Germans began another noisy Ping-Pong game and broke the mood. Dane went back inside. Robin was asleep. His mouth was open and a little gurgling sound came occasionally from his throat, like a small animal drowning. She lay down on her bed and began a new science fiction novel, one John had recommended. She liked it immediately. There was a future civilization which graded people according to their awareness and intelligence. And the more widely you allowed your intelligence to play upon the situations around you, the higher your grade. A very intelligent man might be only a B grade because he lacked the courage to try new things with his intelligence. Suddenly, on another colonial planet, a mystifying problem arose. Things began vanishing. Clothes disintegrated off people's backs. Nobody could build or grow anything. A grade-A man was sent from earth to solve the problem. . . .

John came in, looking radiant and a bit foolish, the look he got when he'd made some discovery. He closed the door gently behind him with an air of mystery.

"You look awfully smug. Have you just made love with Penelope, or something?" she asked.

"No, but I had this . . . rather marvelous thing happen." Her irony had been completely lost on him. "As a matter of fact, Penelope found herself a boyfriend. I left them at Pedro's, dancing. This . . . thing happened when I was walking back alone."

"Who is he? What's he like?" She had come to dread his rather marvelous things. They were usually horribly personal and made her recoil from him.

"His name is Karl. He's a Dutch artist. Very smooth fellow. He appeared at the bar. We were ordering some kind of rum drink she wanted and the bartender didn't understand and this Karl fellow suddenly came up and turned on the charm and cleared things up. He'd been watching her for some time, I think, only he thought we were together. As soon as he found out we weren't . . . you know, you should have seen him set to work."

"Well, I'm glad. I was beginning to get worried that she wouldn't find anybody. This place is not exactly crawling with young, beautiful people," Dane said. Then she added dutifully, "Well, tell me about . . . your thing."

He brightened and came and sat down on

her bed. "On the walk back," he began, like a story, "I decided to cut through a little pine forest. Well, I got lost and ended up in a field, near some stables. I wasn't upset, because I soon reoriented myself. But I thought I might as well roam around: the field was all lit up with moonlight. I walked on, mulling over things, until I came to this remarkable tree. It was very old and thick and—well, I want to get this exact for you. Try and imagine a person, a body, which exudes the maximum comfort, an ageless wisdom, the utmost security, and you'll have some idea. Its branches were profuse. Some of them curled down toward the earth and made a kind of haven for anyone who sat under it. Which I found I suddenly wanted to do. I leaned back against the warm trunk and sat there, looking at the moon through the branches. Then I realized that the moon had begun to exert a gentle, but definite, hypnotic pull on me. There was this tension between us. It was as if the moon were enticing me away from the earth. I thought: Okay, I'll let myself go and see what happens. And I did. I felt myself being pulled away; I was moving toward the moon. I had almost relinquished myself completely—I felt the loosening of gravity around my body—when suddenly I thought: Wait! You're not ready to do this thing yet. You've got things left to do as an individual before you join that . . . cosmic force. Whatever the force was, I was sure it allowed no egos. One would go on living, but transformed. So I put on the brakes. It didn't want to let me go. So I held onto the tree and willed it to anchor me and it did. It was incredible! I could feel the moon and the tree battling it out for me! I closed my eyes and held on for dear life. Then I blacked out. Just before, there had been pain and an unberable dizziness. When I came to, it was with an utter sense of peace—of being accepted completely, at last. I was lying completely curled round the tree, which seemed to be mothering me with its great warmth. And I'd had an ejaculation."

"Oh! God! Why did you have to tell me that? Why did you?" She made a noise of disgust and turned away. Robin moaned in his sleep.

"It was one of the important moments of my life. I want you to know all of these moments. Otherwise, what's the point." But his face had gone white with her rejection.

"They make me love you less."

"Ah, well!" He looked rather disappointed in her. "I'm sorry. You would like to know parts of me, but not all. In that case, tell me: which parts do you wish to know? Tell me how much you can't take."

"You make me sound like a coward."

"I'm trying very hard not to think that."

"Would it really be compromising our perfect marriage if you spent more time displaying your attractive qualities and left the inner mess for yourself, to tinker with in your spare time?"

"You don't seem to distinguish between mess and the natural disorder that precedes growth," he retorted angrily. "Where is the girl who wanted visions, who could cite with such relish the crises of great saints? What kind of mess was it when Saint Paul fell off his horse and writhed in the dust and stood up a transformed man? I suppose that disgusts you, too."

"You have all the saints on your side. I know that. Intellectually. But I still feel disgust. And it separates me from you. Saint Paul knew better than to come home and tell his wife. He knew better, for the sort of man he was, than to take a wife."

John got up. He walked to the door leading to their balcony and took a deep breath of air. "Well, we have taken each other," he said. "What do we do about that?" His lips had gone thin as a line, he showed her a remote profile, left the word to her.

"Couldn't we—don't bite my head off— couldn't we behave more like the Victorians? I mean, they gave dignity and form to their marriages. They respected each other's privacy, put their best foot forward—"

"Oh, by all means, let's do go back a hundred years. There's my brave Dane. Look here," he said passionately. "I didn't marry in order to restrict myself, but to extend myself. Didn't you see what I was offering, what you could offer me? No man knows his own dimensions. He's like the iceberg, he *is* much further than he realizes. That's why the love of another, an equal, can be so creative. It allows him to exist through his partner in new ways of relationship to the world. It gives him another viewpoint from which to see everything, including himself. If I try, as you say you want me to do, to present myself to you like a shopwindow filled only with the choice merchandise, the whole point is gone. What I'm displaying is less than I know myself to be. I am shrinking myself to win your love."

"I can't think," she said, pressing her palms to her temples. "I hear your words, but they have stopped making sense."

"You know what that is," he said, "as well as I."

"I wish I were someone else, far, far away," she said.

"Ah!" He turned away from her and thrust his chin stubbornly toward the black sky outside. To its stars and his temptress moon he said, "I would rather go unloved the rest of my life than to limit myself in order to win an off-center love."

"Off-center," she repeated vaguely. A sudden breeze blew up from the inlet and brought to their room the music from someone's transistor radio. A clear tenor crooned in an American accent:

"I'll be seeing you
  In every lovely summer's day
  In everything that's light and gay
  I'll always think of you that way . . ."

She wondered if her parents had ever danced to that song, early in their marriage during the excitement of the war, before they came to despise each other. She wished she could be Penelope for the rest of the evening, dancing with a brand-new lover who might be everything, her mouth pressed to the warm shoulder of his shirt.

"All I want is truth," John said to the sky.

"All I want is sleep," she said.

Chapter
Six

The Frenchwoman rose gracefully from her towel. She padded across the beach to Dane.

"Do you mind if I sit down?" she asked.

"Please do!" said Dane, making a place for her. There was a wonderful lemony smell about the woman's arms and shoulders. "Oh, what is that lovely smell? Is that a perfume?" Dane asked.

"No, it is a personal suntanning cream I have made up specially," the other replied. "It facilitates tanning while doing wonderful things to the skin. I will have a little supply of it sent to your room, if you think you would like it."

"I'd love that," said Dane. "Tell me, I'm curious: Mrs. Hart told me you and your husband spoke no English, yet here you are speaking to me."

"Ah!" The beautiful Frenchwoman tossed back her hair and laughed. "We pretend to speak only French to avoid talking to people who don't promise to be interesting. But I have been observing you for a week now and decided to break my rule."

"Do you mind if I ask you some things?" Dane said, very much looking forward to this conversation.

"Ask anything you wish!"

"What is the secret of your beautiful life?"

"That is simple. It's only a matter of—"

No, goddamn it, no. She would not wake up. She pressed her face into the pillow, straining to hear the Frenchwoman's answer as it faded into the unreachable realm. But she couldn't get it. What might it have been? Lying there, eyes tightly shut, she tried to work it out intellectually: "That is simple. It's only a matter of"—only a matter of what? Simplicity? Luck? Shit.

She opened her eyes and came to terms with the day. The room was the silvery color of predawn. John was not in his bed. Presently the slight scrape of the metal legs of a chair on the balcony located him for her. Out there writing already. He'd sat up half the night in the bathroom; she had heard his pen, scratch-scratching away, covering the foolscap, undoubtedly, with his tree experience and D's reaction to it. John needed less sleep than any human she'd ever come across. Oh God. Soon it would be time to get up, dress the child, go down to breakfast, get through another holiday. The Frenchwoman would not cross the beach to tell her the secret, either. God.

She decided not to begin the day until,

lying there, asleep for all intents and purposes, she could think of one thing to look forward to. What, in her life, could she be glad about? What did she value, truly value, in it? Penelope's silly exclamation of envy in the customs building goaded her: "I wish *I* could go to a new country to work and within a year find a brilliant man who wanted to marry me and a ready-made little son who had my eyes and didn't even have to have his diapers changed anymore." Words. Their deceptive opacity. Look through them and their real meaning began to shine darkly. New? What had she found new in that ossified country? Stale habits, ancient cultural patterns, a system of manners guaranteed watertight against any gesture of spontaneity. Work? What *real* work that mattered to anyone had she done? Brilliant? Well, yes. But where did you draw the line between genius and crackpot? Marry? Was this gnawing, unfulfilled state called marriage? Ready-made little *son?* More like victimizer, critic, silent little judge. How could you call him child? Cutting deeper into her disillusionment, she discovered that much of her, the virgin territory which once had contained possibilities of infinite growth and joy, was beginning to decay at the edges. A former capacity for hope had turned into a cheap craving for sensation. Herself dulled, she needed sharper stimuli. Before she married John, she was able to engage all the powers of her mind with the sixteen volumes of Proust, keep track of innumerable involutions of sensibility and abstractions in novels and works of philosophy. Now she could not. She read only science fiction and horror stories—and, of course, John's jottings about her. All but the last often put her to sleep. Formerly she had daydreamed entirely of herself doing beautiful, heroic things; now she often daydreamed of doing morbid things. If she could not, for instance, strut a foreign beach with physical assurance, like the Frenchwoman, she *could*, perhaps, retreat wholly into herself, abdicate from her disappointments through various aberrations. With a perverse energy, she pictured a woman lying by herself at one end of the house, coming out only after her husband (and child) were asleep, doing their laundry and preparing their meals for the next day, their ghostly housekeeper. They could have everything from her but the sight of her. Or she saw a woman who sat in a chair all day stuffing herself with sweets and pastries until she achieved a disgusting layer of fat which would keep the world away. Dane with fat pendulous breasts drooping toward a mound of swollen belly and thick haunches: the image produced a strange thrill. John would be below with a patient, his office door closed, and she would sneak downstairs, slowly, ponderously, carrying all her flesh, to admit her lover: a laborer—no, a really grotesque menial, some teeth missing and dirt under the nails. She laid her hand tentatively between her legs, imagining the lewdly sensual ascent of the menial with his fat lady to her, John's, bedroom. He would take off his clothes, smelling of slums, and—

prefacing his act with insults and obscenities —plow his way through the folds and folds of unnatural fat. . . .

No! She would loathe herself afterward.

What, what then? She must have a structure, rules, to get through her day. If nothing else, she must have a system to look forward to. If she could *withdraw*, yes. But not through something self-diminishing like obesity. Through dignity. Yes. That was satisfying and self-preserving: to pull herself tight as a drawstring pouch, preserve what was already inside, allow nothing more to go in or out. "You haven't closed down," said the interesting young doctor standing in her kitchen doorway. "That's what I like about you." Of course not close down, while great things were possible. But when they ceased to be: shut the lid and lock it from below and keep yourself to yourself. Her father had done this, in a way. Bitch of a wife ran out on him all the time, finally ran out for good. He neither moaned her loss nor left himself open for another like her. He simply pulled himself a little tighter than he was before, threw all his energies into the keeping and polishing of what he had. He taught his daughter to be clean and proud, taught his students the art of war at sea, and in his spare time managed to produce a terse and accurate little monograph on one of the few subjects overlooked by all the other Civil War historians. *The Unsung Brothers Tift* it was called, and told the much neglected story of the obscure brothers, two New Orleans shipbuilders who had put their finest energies and talents into the making of a ship which was to win the war for the South, had it not been necessary for them to consent to its being blown up before the maiden voyage to keep the Yankees from getting it.

Robin whined from his cot. He wanted to get up, but wouldn't until somebody came for him. A minute more. She pushed her mouth, nose, closed eyes for just a minute more into the pillow, constructed a very temporary set of images by which to guide her day: perfect monographs, cold clean water, Mr. von Schirmbeck's dive, dove-gray English Rollses whisking silently through nasty weather, windows sealed against a molecule of intrusion; Marcus Aurelius, Queen Elizabeth on horseback at the trooping of the colors, monks writing with frozen fingers in chilly monasteries, Jane Austen's world of manners. She would be Victorian. Silent. Circumscribed. Closed.

At breakfast, Penelope said, "Dane, you've got to go with me this morning, to support me."

"Where?"

"To the stables. Karl—this Dutchman—has asked me to ride. He is great friends with the man who owns it. He's a count or something."

"Who, Karl?"

"No, the man who owns the horses. I haven't ridden in four years—not since coming to London. I'm afraid I'll be a flop and he'll regret asking me. I told him you were coming; he wants to meet you."

"I'm sure he does."

John came out of his remoteness long enough to say, "Why don't you go? Robin might enjoy seeing the horses."

"What are you going to do?"

"Finish up some notes. Then work on my idea. Go for a swim." He sounded quite pleased at the prospects of his day.

"It's all the same to me," Dane told Penelope. Then, remembering her images, she addressed her stepson coolly and cordially: "Robin, how would you like to go and see some horses?" And when he only looked at her with the blue eyes, she said, "Good. I thought you'd like it."

Leaving the hotel, they met Mrs. Hart coming back from her morning walk. She wore enormous knee-length shorts and brogues and high socks. Her freckled hands wer filled with seashells, ferns and assorted flowers.

"*There's* the little man," she said, handing Robin a yellow flower. To everyone's surprise he took it.

"Say 'Thank you,' Robin," coaxed Penelope. Dane could have slapped her. Under the new rules, she was going to treat his silence as commonplace. Robin, of course, said nothing. Dane smiled at Mrs. Hart and said, "That's very kind of you. We're off to the riding stables. Penelope is going to ride with a friend."

"Ah, Count Bartolomé." Mrs. Hart nodded. "He is a nice man. Well, have a lovely day. Good-bye, darling," and she backed away, waving at Robin, who turned to watch her.

Penelope hurried along, down the dusty

road. The scenery drowsed in the morning heat. The sky was a pitiless, even blue.

"Do these trousers look all right? If only I'd thought to bring my riding breeches!"

"They look fine. There's nothing sexier than tight, faded jeans," said Dane. "They make it look as though you're not trying."

"Oh, *sexy*," trilled Penelope nervously. She flushed. Dane hurried beside her, dragging Robin. She tried to imagine having something to hurry toward on this island. She couldn't.

They came to the crossroads and a meadow spotted with old trees. Dane saw several likely candidates for John's experience, and looked away. On the other side, beyond a low stone wall, some sun-blackened laborers were building a house.

"How archaic," said Penelope. "Look at those flimsy sticks holding up the ceiling. No girders, nothing. How long do you think it takes them to finish a house?"

"Months. I don't know. Forever." The sun was beginning to give her a headache. Robin wanted to stop and watch the men at work. He grunted officiously and pulled her to a halt beside the wall. A dark man pushing a wheelbarrow saw them. He grinned and waved wildly at the boy. *"Hola, hermoso!"* As he waved and called, he continued pushing his barrow up a steep wooden incline. He forgot to watch his footing and almost fell. "Ayee!" he cried in mock terror, and righted himself. Dane imagined him smashing to the ground, blood everywhere, and the child watching, cool and bemused.

Karl was there. He was good-looking with the sharpish, golden Northern Europe looks, and carried himself with a precise casualness. He wore neat riding breeches and high boots which looked new. His dark-blue shirt was left open halfway down his chest, revealing a field of pale gold hair. He was not the sort of man who interested Dane: too much the magazine-model type with none of the dark undercurrents about him. He did have a certain foxy something, however, which made her respectfully wary of him. He and an older, swarthy man in faded riding clothes stood together by the stables, talking to each other and openly watching the approach of the two women. The swarthy man was at least fifty, but Dane much preferred his style. Of course he must be the Count. There was authentic aristocracy in the worn quality of the clothes. Nevertheless, she was glad Penelope had found herself a handsome boyfriend. The two of them would go well together on the beach, with their golden looks.

Penelope introduced Karl to Dane. He said, "Oh, the doctor's wife," looking at her curiously as he shook hands.

Count Bartolomé had better manners. He put out his cigarette, grinding it into the dust beneath his heel, swaggered forward on rather bowed legs, kissed Dane's hand, then Penelope's. Then he saw Robin.

Curling back his lips into a huge tobacco-stained smile, he pronounced, "Without a doubt, señora, the most handsome little Englishman I have ever seen. Is true. You are a proud woman to have such a son, no?"

"Thank you," said Dane, wishing Penelope were not there to spoil her gratification by knowing the truth.

"*Oye!*" he said to Robin, rocking back on his heels. "I tell you what. Maybe you ride one of my ponies later. Eh, *caballero?* You would like that?"

Robin stared at the Count.

"He's sometimes shy with strangers." Dane began the old refrain, forgetting her new rules for a moment in the presence of this forceful man. What had Penelope told Karl about her and Robin and John? Not anything, she hoped. She did not like the idea of that wily blond man knowing anything about her life.

"*Es precoz,* that is all," said the Count, turning to Karl. "He is—how you say?—'adding me up.' I like that. I bet you do not speak to just anyone, eh, *hijo?*" looking back at the child.

"No, he doesn't," said Dane.

"*Bueno.* Karl, we get horses, eh? Pepe! *Preparalos la yegua y Pirata!*"

"Has Pirata been ridden today?" asked Karl.

"No, I save him for you. Only two, three persons I trust to Pirata and his moods."

"He only needs understanding," replied the Dutchman with a wry smile. He winked toward Penelope, who flushed, swallowed and looked away.

"Understanding. Yes." The Count chuckled softly. "And, señorita, you shall ride my Serafina. Look there, Pepe is bringing her now."

He pointed out a stall with his imperious short brown fingers. Everyone turned to watch the groom lead a splendid palomino mare into the open air. Her body blazed golden as she stepped tentatively into the sun, a thatch of champagne-colored mane dipping demurely forward over one eye. Her steps were careful, deliberate, anticipatory. There was an exquisite tension in her as though she looked forward to something.

"That is my darling," said the Count with much feeling. He went to the mare as if drawn to her light. He murmured in Spanish, stroking her, his dark stubby fingers lingering on her soft muzzle. Dane couldn't stop watching him touch the mare. And when he stood by to steady her when Pepe heaved the saddle on her, Dane saw the Count's spine flinch with the mare's.

It took both Pepe and Karl to saddle Pirata. The bay's nostrils flared dramatically; he had to be tugged from his stall. He seemed to know a performance was expected of him. Russet coils of light shot down his flanks when they fastened the strap under his belly. The mare's ears went up; her back was to the stallion.

In a flash, Karl mounted him, clenching the huge body in his scissors grip. His new boots gleamed. The count helped Penelope mount, steadying her tennis shoe in the stirrup as she swung up on the gold mare.

"All set?" called the Dutchman. He turned in his saddle to give the girl a quirky, private smile. Then he nudged the stallion into the ring. Lowering her head, the mare followed.

"*Despacio*," cautioned the Count. "Go a little slow at first, Karl." He threw forward his pelvis and flicked his crop against the rail. It was Penelope he was anxious about. He watched her, frowning, until she fell into a natural rhythm with his prize mare. "Ah," he sighed, relaxing and turning to Dane. "She rides just beautifully, señora." He said it as though it were a compliment to herself. Feeling that he approved of her, she went to sit on the bench near where he stood. Robin stayed behind, playing at the water trough. He devised a game, throwing in the yellow flower Mrs. Hart had given him, watching it float, pulling it out again. He makes a ritual out of all his play, thought Dane.

"*Te diviertes, hijo?*" the Count asked him. "What is your son's name, please, señora?"

"Robin."

"Robin. I never hear that before. Hey, *pajarito*, you know what I am going to do? Eh? I am going to let you ride my Serafina when the lady has finish. What do you say?"

"I don't think he's ever ridden," Dane said, thinking too late: "I don't *think*": what kind of statement is that for a mother to make?

"Is no matter, señora. It is perfectly safe, I can assure you. My own grandchildren ride Serafina. She herself is gentle as a little child." He seemed adamant that his gift be accepted.

"Oh, it's fine with *me*," Dane said quickly. "If he'll go."

"Ho! Not go! For a ride on Serafina?"

Hearing himself discussed, Robin had

halted beside the water trough. He listened intently.

"Why, no child has ever refuse a ride on Serafina," said the Count. "It is a special honor. Of course Robin will ride. Yes, Robin?"

The boy turned his full blue gaze upon the man.

"Oof, I am stricken!" cried the Count, grabbing his stomach and sinking to the ground so authentically that Dane started up from her bench. "Oh, I am stricken, I am dying under that block-of-ice look."

A queer twisted expression came on Robin's face. His mouth contorted into an unnatural shape. He forced his lips together and clenched his small fists at his sides. Oh God, what kind of scene was he going to make now?

"*Poor* Señor Bart," moaned the Count, his legs buckling comically in his boots. He looked just like the dying hero in a Western melodrama. "Those chilly eyes like a knife in his heart. Robin is killing a poor old man. Ah . . . ahhh . . . ah? Ah-ha? Come on now, I got you. Yes "

To Dane's amazement, Robin's contorted mouth broke into a delighted, childlike smile. But he covered it immediatey with both small hands and turned away, distressed.

"I think I have won him," the Count said casually. He turned back to the ring, not pushing the game further.

A careful duet was in progress between the riders and their mounts. Karl and Pirata initiated the gait; Penelope and Serafina followed suit. Dane fell into a sort of trance, watching them go round and round. Anchored in substantial sensations—dry heat on skin, the squeak of leather as the riders rose and fell in their saddles, the smell of horseflesh and tobacco —she began to relax.

Count Bartolomé came and sat beside her. "A splendid sight, two beautiful animals in agreement," he said.

"Yes, that's true," she replied.

"Do you ride, señora?"

"No. My father gave me lessons, but I never could learn. The horse and I never seemed to get together."

"Ah, that is a shame. I am sure I could teach you. I would first get you to feel the extensions of the horse: the way he moves, the way he *is*. All the technique, that is second. Anybody can teach the curve of the leg, the holding of the reins, that's nothing. One must first get in harmony."

"Yes, in harmony," Dane repeated, chewing on her lower lip.

"How long you going to be here?"

"Only one more week, I'm afraid."

"I give you a few lessons, perhaps, señora. You would like it. It is something—oh—*free*, to be riding. You could lose yourself in it. And you are very tall. You would look elegant on a horse, I think."

"Oh, I couldn't learn," laughed Dane. "Horses just ignore me when I get on them. They start eating grass."

The Count laughed, showing all his small,

tobacco-stained teeth. "Then you must make him *stop* eating grass." His black eyes danced at her from their crinkly pouches. He was flirting a little and they both knew it.

"I guess so," she said. "Well, perhaps—"

"Who is *this,* creeping up like a little mouse!" he cried. For Robin had inched up on them unobtrusively, his eyes on the Count. "Yes, you know your time is coming, don't you, *hijo?* Soon you will be sitting high in the air on Serafina. Almost touching the sunshine, you will be so high. Eh? I will walk close beside you, the better to see those blue eyes. You and me and Serafina, won't that be nice?" He flicked his crop against his boot as he spoke. Robin watched, mesmerized.

When Penelope had dismounted, she joined Dane on the bench.

"I'm going to be sore, I can feel it already," she said.

"What does it matter? It will be worth it for looking so good."

"You are sweet," cried the girl, squeezing Dane's arm. She was full of herself. Her skin glowed and she exuded vitality. Out of the corner of her eye she was watching Karl as he rubbed down Pirata.

The Count directed Pepe in shortening the stirrups of Serafina's saddle.

"I had forgotten the thrill of riding," said Penelope. "It lifts me right up. All those months in London when I was so depressed! All I had to do was go down to Hyde Park and rent a horse. Why didn't I think of it? All that moping around."

"Perhaps you didn't want to be lifted up at the time."

"My gosh, Dane, look at Robin."

Count Bartolomé led the child toward the mare, who stood with lowered head. The groom held her bridle.

"*Primero*," the Count was saying gently, "we shall say hello to her. See how she puts down her head? That is because she wants you to touch her face." He lifted the child as if he weighed nothing and brought Serafina's muzzle to meet his shy hand. "Yes! Good. Touch her. Oh, she likes that. Up and down her nose. Isn't it soft and nice? She says you may sit on her if you like. Ooof! No, one leg at a time. Good. Very good."

Momentarily, the little boy hovered on the edge of panic. He was so high above the ground, astride the big animal. But the Count was there beside him. Hypnotically, he spoke into the child's puckered face.

"How nice it must be up there. How I envy you. Is it nice, *hijo?*"

Robin nodded once.

The Count took hold of the bridle and walked the mare around the ring very slowly. He talked nonstop to the boy, who gradually relaxed. Dane was touched by the tenderness in the man's voice. Robin's feet in the little red shoes went flop-flop-flop in the shortened stirrups.

"*Más rápidamente*, I think. You want we go a *tiny* bit faster?"

Robin nodded. If only John could see him now! Presently, his little rump beat up and down in the saddle. His mouth formed the same O as when John tossed him high in the air, but behind the O was the hint of a smile.

"Your son is a born rider!" Count Bartolomé called to her, steadying the child's back with his hand. It was necessary for him to trot beside the horse to keep up. Dane suddenly remembered John saying of Vanessa: "A natural country girl. She'd been brought up with horses and loved to ride." "You bring him a couple more times and I get him started good. You, too, señora."

After they had gone round a few more times, the Count slowed the mare. When at last they were at a standstill, he said to Robin, lifting him from the horse, "You had your first ride, didn't you? You like to come back again and see Serafina?"

Robin nodded vigorously.

"You shall! Now we go and see your mother."

Robin stopped dead still.

"Come on," said the Count, offering his hand.

The child began to shriek. He stood rigid, his feet planted hard in the dust of the ring.

"Stop that now, Robin," she said, edging toward him. A sticky film seemed to move down over her vision.

"Look, now. Here is your mother." The Count picked the child from the ground and made ready to transfer him to Dane. Robin screamed, flailing the red shoes wildly. He landed a blow square in the man's groin. The

Count bent double with pain and embarrassment.

"I am sorry, señora," he could barely croak. "I have cause some trouble." He did not look at her, and only just managed to keep his hands from going to comfort himself.

She felt herself, at this point, cut loose from all shame. She had a task, that was all. This screaming red thing must be plucked like a leech from the scene and gotten away.

"He often has these fits," she said, her voice hard. As if it were a game, she managed to snatch off one little shoe, then the other, from the kicking feet. Feeling almost gay, she hauled the creature over her hip. Now he could kick only the sunlit air. "Thank you for your kindness," she said, and turned and began walking toward the road, carrying the little red shoes and the red screaming child. No more riding lessons for anybody.

"Shall I come, too?" Penelope called anxiously.

"Good heavens, what for?" Dane returned, without looking round. She heard the Dutchman mutter, "But what has upset him so?" A silence followed. Oh, let old Penelope say what she pleased. Besides, who could stop anyone from saying anything?

As she lugged him hurriedly up the dusty road, his shrieks turned to sobs. No, she could never depend on him to carry on the Victorian farce. He thrashed like a dying fish at her hip and every one of the construction crew stopped to stare at the sight: grim-faced woman striding along with wailing English child. Let the sun-blackened peons criticize. She felt as hard as a tank, moving across the battlefield. Trees wavered steamily before her eyes. Which tree was John's tree? Where was her ecstasy now?

When they reached the hotel, he had given up all noise but little moans of protest. In the courtyard, she slipped him from her aching body. Her dress was soaking wet all down the side he'd been on. He stood below her in his socks, his red and puckered face set against her. Water trickled down his legs.

"You little bastard," she said between her teeth. Then she spotted Ramírez-Suárez watching, just inside the door. Sighing, she bent down and collected Robin in her arms. Spent from his fit, he didn't resist. "Poor thing, you're all tired," she crooned, nuzzling his face. She carried him past the smiling manager. "We've had an exhausting morning," she said. She managed to preserve her front up three flights of stairs, even after there was no one to see.

Chapter
Seven

John was writing on the balcony. He looked, shaded by the big umbrella, as though the day had not yet touched him. "Has he been crying?" he said, when she came out to see what was doing and the child followed.

"Brilliant deduction. All women should marry geniuses."

"Did anything happen?" he asked carefully.

"Oh, nothing much. He rode this horse and kicked a man in the balls when he had to get off."

"I'm afraid you've lost me," John said. He capped his pen with a hardly audible sigh. (". . . affecting reponsibility," she read among the cluttered black scribble.) He pushed aside the heap of papers and laced his long pale fingers on the tabletop. "Suppose you sit down and tell me what's happened. What's this about his riding? He's never been on a horse in his life."

"He has now. The man who owns the stable took a fancy to his snobbishness. He insisted upon putting him up on his best palomino mare."

"And you didn't think this was dangerous?" Robin skulked beside his father, listening to himself being discussed. With his pink eyes and spotted face, he looked like a little wounded animal set against her.

"Oh, Robin is a born rider. The Count said so. I guess he gets it from his mother. You should have seen Robin respond to this man, John. I've never seen him get along with anyone so well. Not even you."

"He kicked him in the balls, you said."

"That was afterward. He was having a fit because he had to return to his wicked stepmother."

"Oh dear. I do wish we could work out—"

"I'm going to have a bath now."

"You're always taking baths. Or going to sleep. Dane, do you want this holiday to succeed?"

"I don't know what I want." A perverse calm filled her. She sat down at the table. Maybe he'll tell me what I want, she thought.

He said, "I made some notes on what happened last night. I understand you much better now. Would you like to see them?"

Openly offered like this, the prospect repelled her. But what new things had he learned about her? She couldn't bear not knowing. "Okay," she said.

"They're just here." He ruffled through the papers, looking pleased, the way he did when they set out together somewhere: to dinner, a movie. He handed her a sheet filled with his crabbed writing. The whole page was about her. What a find this would have been, had she purloined it from his suitcase!

"Like me," she began to read, "she has always dreamed of evolution, pioneering." She looked up to meet his dark moist eyes behind the glasses. "I can't concentrate with you staring at me, John."

"Sorry." He turned his attention to Robin. "Hello there," he said heartily, swinging the pouty child onto his lap. "Mommy says you went for a nice ride on a horse."

The child shook his head no.

"He's bloody lying," she said, reading on:

The books she reads, the things that interest her most, reflect this. But she manages to keep this side of herself in the realm of possibility, safely insulated from her practical life, so that one cannot alter the other. She likes to dream of transformation. The difficulty arises when I come along and tell her it's true. When I begin to demonstrate it, she panics and revolts. When I remind her that I married her with every intention of doing these things with her, she retreats at once behind the traditions she swears she wants to transcend. Torn between wanting to accompany me and "see what I see," she chooses a halfway house, remaining at home among her props of convention and waiting for me to report back on my discoveries—censoring the less agreeable parts.

"It's interesting," she said, getting up. "I really must take a bath now."

"But what do you think? Do you agree or not?"

"I don't know. Like I said, it's interesting. But it doesn't ring any bells. It doesn't generate anything."

"You haven't given it a chance to! Why can't we discuss it?" He was practically out of his chair. He seemed incredulous that she could walk away. This "walking away" had been the cause of their first terrible argument just after they were married. John's mother had come to London for her twice-a-year shopping trip. Mrs. Empson, now a widow, had exiled herself to the Isle of Man to avoid John's having to pay duties on *her* death. She had not yet met her son's wife, and so it had been arranged by letter that the three of them should dine at Mrs. Empson's hotel. Dane dressed carefully for this meeting with her mother-in-law. She was fully prepared to be quizzed about herself, her interests, her education, her impressions of England and her hopes for John. She knew John and his mother had had a serious break in relations when he decided not to become a Jesuit and had subsequently left the church. His mother blamed the whole thing on Oxford, John had told Dane, and had once said she wished she could bomb the place. Dane imagined herself being the instrument of a reconciliation between mother and son. She had a knack, she knew, for making older people approve of her. But she was not prepared for the fullness of their estrangement. It had been the most uncomfortable meal of her life. Mother and son addressed each other with the polite reticence of strangers (British strangers) forced to share a table. At no point during the meal was there a single allusion to a shared past, a single mention of the personal life of either. When they talked, haltingly, sometimes all beginning at once after a long silence, it was about the weather, the London traffic, a currently sensational case running at the Old Bailey, which Mrs. Empson was following, and some rather gruesome traffic accidents, the details of which were recounted in a soft, matter-of-fact voice by this small woman with diamonds in her ears. Dane's achievement of the evening was getting Mrs. Empson to admit she shared with her daughter-in-law a predilection for Arthur Machen's horror stories. Several times, Dane caught the older woman stealing wistful glances at her son, who did not seem to notice. He had gone abstract very early in the meal and remained so until she announced over her first cigarette after dinner that she should be going to bed. Not once had she mentioned her son's marriage. She showed no sign of either approval or disapproval.

Dane thought John should have brought the subject up himself, led into it simply and casually. She told him so later when they were having a bath together before bed.

"I think you could have tried harder," Dane said. They sat face to face in the tub, knees touching. "It's obvious she loves you. She kept looking at you."

"She gave me up years ago. We have nothing to say to each other now."

"There were a lot of things you could have said. If I had been you, I would simply have begun talking about my marriage—you know, what we do, setting up house, anything. Make her feel part of it."

"She doesn't want to feel part of it. She couldn't. She doesn't know the me who married you. She isn't capable of it, doesn't want to. Her son was to be somebody altogether different."

"Oh well. You're probably right. Anyway, she's *your* mother. Thank God for Arthur Machen, all the same. He saved the evening." Dane got out of the tub and began drying herself.

"You can't leave," he had all but screamed, his face going darker by the second. "You can't just walk out on something like this."

"Don't be silly. Who's walking out? The water was getting cold. Besides, I don't know anything about her anyway. What more was there to say?"

He splashed out of the tub and followed her naked through the house, dripping water on the carpet. "It's irresponsible," he accused, sitting down on their bed almost in tears. She had never seen him like this. It frightened and repulsed her.

"You're getting the bed wet," she said. "Listen, I'm exhausted. I'm not used to *that* degree of British reserve. If there's anything to talk about, can't we do it tomorrow?"

"Tomorrow will be too late; it's *alive* now," he said. A circle of wetness spread wider on the bedspread beneath his pale haunches. She grew more and more agitated at the sight

118

of him sitting there naked, pleading, expecting *what* of her?

"Oh God," she cried suddenly. "Oh *God!*"

"What's the matter?" he asked, looking alarmed for her.

She began hitting the side of her head with her fist hard. She whacked at her head and screamed, "Oh God oh God oh God," like a madwoman. He got up from the bed and snatched away her fist.

"Stop that, you'll concuss yourself. You're hysterical," he said. She could hear him coming back, the solicitous physician, the capable, austere man she had married. It was he who ended the evening consoling her, sitting beside the bed and stroking her head until she dropped off to sleep.

Now she said, "I can't think until I have a bath and wash off this terible morning. I carried that screaming child for half a mile. He peed on me. Look—here. I haven't even changed my dress. Let me have a bath before I try to discuss this thing you wrote."

"Oh dear. I am sorry. Robin, have you been a trial? By all means, go and have a bath. Perhaps there'll be time before lunch."

"Perhaps," she said, feeling more cheerful at the reprieve. "Maybe I'll have some ideas about it in the tub. Look at Archimedes."

She went inside, leaving them behind. The room was cool. She stood in front of the mirror, biting her lip and thinking. Then, on an impulse, she quickly changed her dress, took up her purse and went quietly out of the room and down the stairs. She hurried like a fugitive from the hotel, feeling daring and rather naughty.

She had lunch at Pedro's all by herself, sitting under a shady tree, with plenty of space all around her. She ordered a rum Coke, then another. The day began to melt pleasantly around her contours. It would do them good to be without her for a while. Two old women, dressed in black, came out of the church across the street. She watched them hobble off down the shop-lined street, moving like omens of mortality among the tourist trade. She decided to go across the street and have a look inside the church.

Bitter incense and ecclesiastical gloom enveloped her like a friend. Nobody else was in the pews. Catholic churches with all their iconography fascinated her. She'd never been taken to church, as her father did not believe in God. He believed in things you could see and virtues you could practice. His heroes were Marcus Aurelius and Robert E. Lee. The one time she had seen moisture in his eyes was when he read aloud to her the General's farewell to his troops. Captain Tarrant's favorite virtue was suffering defeat or setback with a quiet dignity. When Dane was three, her mother had walked out on them for good. It was a sunny Saturday morning in spring. While Dane watched through the window and saw her mother put her suitcases into a big car, helped by a big, jolly-looking man, her father went from room to room collecting pairs of shoes—

his and Dane's. She heard him spread news-papers on the kitchen table as the big car drove away.

"Do you know what day this is?" he called from the kitchen. She heard the unlatching of the wooden box, the setting out of brushes, the *ting* of his penny opening a tin of Kiwi Boot Polish. Her favorite event of the week was this very time. She got down from the window, feeling guilty that she looked forward to it just as much as ever. And it was so peace-ful with her mother gone.

"Shoe polishing day!" she cried, running to him. She decided to cry later, perhaps that night, for the loss of her mother. But that night they went to a seafood restaurant for dinner and to a movie afterward. Gene Kelly, wearing bell bottoms, tap-danced through Paris.

She wandered down a side aisle, brows-ing among the stations of the cross. A thin, masochistic-looking Christ dragged deter-minedly toward his hill. She sat down beneath his plaster-of-paris crucifixion. The pew smelled of fresh wax. Maybe she ought to leave John, start again. But where? How? She couldn't go back to the meaningless editorial waiting game so many girls played at, in publishers' offices all over the world. Waiting for the Big Event. This *was* her Big Event, supposedly. Only, what did you do when it turned out to be not *grand* Big, so you felt yourself expanding, be-ing more than you were before but *stifling* Big, overwhelming—each thing you conceded becoming another deprivation to yourself? She imagined marriage to someone exceptional like John would be like two stars shining separately but equally as bright, outshining those millennia of lesser flickers in a black night. But this other star would not keep his distance. He kept encroaching on her space, trying to collide and merge with her like those horrible zygotes. It reminded her of a Walt Disney movie on reproduction which had been shown to her Girl Scout troop. She had been appalled when the cartoon sperm had whipped himself with a wet resounding *plok!* right smack into the poor defenseless egg. Then, to background music, the awful joined thing began going wild, multiplying like a cancer, until there was no trace left of the two separate things.

"I can understand Lucifer so well!" she once exclaimed to John. "His only crime was wanting to be himself, holding out against becoming a nobody in the cosmic collective farm. What's *wrong* with wanting to preserve your ego from anonymity?"

"The paradox is," he replied calmly, "that when one is most nearly himself, he is quite content to be no one at all. It's only those things we know we *can* lose that we're afraid of losing." Then, characteristically, he added, "Do you see what I mean?"

She hadn't seen, exactly, but his words had reverberated with a promise of some future understanding. Just like those notes about herself she'd read today. His words could send intriguing tracers just beyond where her mind could reach. He was impossible to love, to live with in honor and affection, but who else had she known, would she ever meet, who might know her better than she knew herself? Would you jump ship into lonely waters, unknown (possibly shark-infested), just because the captain had disagreeable habits (watching your every thought with moist brown eyes, dancing in black-stockinged feet to symphonies in the living room, writing down on foolscap the experiences that other people simply *lived*), *if you had the certainty that he and he alone might steer you to your destination?* Which was . . .? Realizing myself, she decided. Fulfilling me, Dane. Being completely myself.

Frowning hard into the incense-laden murk, she met a pair of wise black eyes staring back at her. She practically leaped out of her skin. It was an old priest, spying on her from behind a statue of the Virgin Mary. Momentarily, she expected him to whisk down the isle in his long black soutane and accuse her of something. But when he saw he'd been seen, he hurried away, a quick black wraith, into the restricted sanctity of the chancel. Unnerved, Dane got up and left the church.

She walked without direction for a while, until she came into a very pleasant hilly street, steeped in heavy foliage. High walls surrounded interesting-looking villas whose inhabitants all seemed to be sleeping. As Dane climbed the hill, the muscles pulled tight in her legs and the air became fragrant with the scent of flowers. The crisis of the morning she relegated to some unused corner of her mind, to be taken out and thought about later. She recalled her Victorian resolve upon waking this morning. It might still be possible. She would try harder with John and Robin, acting out the role until it came naturally to her. Perhaps this entire situation was only waiting for her to garnish it with her love and grace. Then: might not John be transformed into a man she could feel passion for? Might not Robin come out of his shell, smile at her with the small milk-white teeth, snuggle up to her, make her proud? How possible it seemed as she walked up the hill beside the lovely villas! It was as though she had already accomplished it.

At the top of the hill, the street suddenly ended without warning. It was a dead end. Beyond it was a final, lone villa which looked out directly over the green sea below. It was a whitewashed stucco with bright scarlet blossoms clambering unchecked up the sides. The front door was of heavy dark oak with carved figures in the panels. At the left corner of the upper story, two adjacent windows were open and Dane could look through the front one, its wispy green curtain blowing like sea hair, and see a view of the sky through the second one. At the right side of the villa, a section of it visible to the road, was a tiled terrace banked by multicolored flowers and humming softly with butterflies and bees. On a candy-striped lounge chair someone had flung a copy of *Réalités*. Its expensive glossy pages whipped languidly in the breeze. The people who must live in such a house . . .

Dane contemplated what they would be

like, when her dream was broken by a raucous female curse. A naked little girl of about two ran onto the terrace as though pursued by furies. A quick, urchinlike woman in a black swimsuit exploded into the picture. "Come here, damn you!" she cried to the child in a funny hoarse voice. "Come here and get what's coming to you!" The two ran round and round the terrace, the child screaming and the woman cursing. Suddenly there was a third member of the little tableau: another naked girl-child, identical to the other. She ran in the wake of the two, emitting little screams of excitement, as though this were a game. The woman stubbed her bare toe on a tile, lost her balance and crashed into the chaise longue. *Réalites* flopped to the ground. The twin girls stopped to watch for a second too long, for she lunged and caught both of them, fastening the one in the grip of her long sturdy legs while she beat the other. When she seemed quite satisfied, she sent the beaten one off with a wail and started almost hungrily on the second. The release she was feeling came, like a tangible presence in the warm air, to Dane, who watched from the road. When the woman had finished, she pushed the child away from her, it wailing as well, and, against the duet of cries, addressed the landscape in general. "It's too fucking much," she announced in her pebbly voice.

Dane began clapping vigorously from the road. The woman looked up, shielding her eyes. The twins stopped their howling.

There was a short silence; then both women began to laugh.

The woman padded across the lawn to Dane. "They were trying to put an ancient old tabby cat into the clothes dryer. I don't mean trying to put, they'd actually got her in—when I got there they were trying to shut the door."

"That would have been a hot cat," Dane said. "But that's children for you. I'm taking the afternoon off from my little boy. I went and drank rum Cokes and then a priest chased me out of the church."

"You are marvelous!" cried the other in her hoarse voice. "You just show up outside the house when I'm beating my kids, and you're American, aren't you? Damn, I haven't spoken *English* with another woman in at least a year. Can you come in and have a drink? Please do! If you do, I'll tell you my life story."

"I'd love to." Dane felt as though she were entering an interesting book.

"Wonderful," said the other. "I'm Polly Heykoop." The name sounded vaguely familiar.

"My name is Dane Empson." She followed the woman back to the terrace, through the thick grass. The twins capered along as well, like naked nymphs with red bottoms.

"*Dane?* What kind of name is that? Like Danes and Norwegians?"

"No. Everybody thinks that. It's rather odd. My father wanted a boy. He was going to name him Daniel. When I came instead, he castrated the name and gave it to me anyway."

"You're out of your mind! I love it. Come into the kitchen. Let me get you another rum and Coke before you sober up."

"It's funny," said Dane. "I was standing out there on the road, admiring your villa. I was trying to imagine the people who must live here."

"Ha. Maybe you should have stayed out there on the road if you wanted to keep your beautiful imaginings. This isn't even our house. It belongs to my husband's best friend, who's rich. Come in."

Dane followed her into a cool, high-ceil-inged interior furnished very sparely with rich-grained Spanish woods and muted woven rugs on the shining parquet floors. The walls were adorned only with several enormous canvases of energetic nude women. They seemed to flow out into the somber room, bringing with them the vibrant golds and oranges of their tresses, warming the cool decor with their peach-toned skins.

"I wish we had one of those in our living room," said Dane. "How I hate the thing we have now: it's a big black-and-white nothing—except it's chilly as hell and sinister."

"Those are my husband's," said Polly. "He's pretty good at women. That's all he paints. He had a showing last year: a hundred and thirty canvases, all nudes. He sold a lot of them. Women are his hobby and his liveli-hood. But he's a good artist. I'm glad of that. It's important to be good at something, I think. That's my trouble: I've got all this energy and nothing to do with it. I've become morbidly interested in personalities because I haven't got anything else to do. All Karl's friends and their wives are scared of me, because I ferret out their little secrets."

"Wait a minute. Your husband isn't Dutch, is he?"

"You've met him already? That doesn't surprise me. He prowls around the island at night and leaves me to babysit."

"I met a blond Dutchman at the riding stables this morning."

"That's him, that's him. He and Bart are thick as thieves. Did he make a pass at you?" She raked short bitten nails through her thatch of black hair and her small dark eyes shone like chips of coal.

"Who? the Count, or—"

"Karl, silly. Don't worry, I won't be mad. He flirts with all pretty women. Then he sleeps with them. Then he paints them and sells the canvases for lots of money to feed his skinny wife and naughty little twins."

"No, he didn't flirt. Honestly. I guess I didn't pass the modeling test." She didn't mention Penelope, but it was interesting to think about: so the holiday lover was a married man. The fact did not displease her.

"Don't be silly, you're beautiful! Come into the kitchen. Another rum and Coke? You seem to flower from them."

The kitchen was chaotic, its sink counter crammed with open jars of baby food, brim-filled ashtrays, stacks of unwashed dishes, a pair of eyebrow tweezers, what looked like a piece of bacon which had been chewed for a while and then spit out, an aerogramme addressed to Herr Karl Heykoop with a German stamp on it, a children's storybook in Dutch and several empty ice trays. A dirty diaper was flung across the open porthole of the washing machine. From a square of sunny floor, a frowsy marmalade cat raised her head briefly to glare at them.

"Aren't you American?" Dane said as Polly sloshed a generous dollop of Bacardi into a glass that could have been cleaner.

"Born in Fairbanks of Polish parents and married to a Dutchman. But I'm American, all right. I would have made a good pioneer woman. I could have coped with the Indians with pleasure. All that space and excitement. Oh, I was hot to get out of boring, sprawling old Fairbanks and come to cultural, interesting Europe. I married my first husband, Randall, just to get out of Fairbanks. He was in the Army and we came to Europe. Now, six years, two marriages and two children later, I've made it to the laundromats of Amsterdam. It's your turn. What does your husband do? Did you come here all the way from America for a holiday?"

"No, we live in London. John is English. He's a psychiatrist." The information evoked its usual instant of respect.

"Wild," said Polly. "I'm trying very hard not to envy you. But"—she giggled raucously —"you probably have your guilty secret. I'll have to work extra hard to find it out. Just kidding; don't take me seriously. Swinging London. Well, that settles it: I've decided we're going to become best friends and then you'll invite me to visit you in London. Hey, that'll be great. I can leave the twins with Karl's mother. She's always complaining she never sees enough of them. I've always wanted to go to the Wax Museum."

"Why not?" said Dane, and she really meant it. She herself could use a friend. And Polly had a nice brittleness to her; Penelope was so bland.

"Come on outside," said Polly. "Is your child a boy or—You said boy. Does he have a nanny?"

They went outside with their drinks. Polly insisted Dane must take the candy-striped lounge chair; she herself sat on the low wall just beside, swinging her long legs like a tomboy.

"No, he hasn't got a nanny," she said thoughtfully, sipping her drink. How strange: a few moments ago, she had been spying on this terrace from the road. Now she was sitting in the candy-striped lounge chair. "We have a woman, though," she added on impulse, "who cares for him. Her name is Mrs. Christopher. She's very devoted to him."

"Gosh." Polly gulped her drink and made a face. "You're lucky. How did you meet your husband? What's he like?

"He was speaking before a group of intellectuals. I went because I was covering the meeting for my magazine. As soon as I saw him sitting there, I said to myself, 'That's for me.' I worked it so he'd take me home."

"I'll bet you worked it," said Polly with admiration. "What's he like?"

Dane looked into the red-brown depths of her glass; she shaped her thoughts. "He's remarkable," she said, frowning. "He's the most intelligent person I've ever met. I'm not saying it's easy to be married to such a person—"

"Easy! It's not easy to be married, period!" cried Polly.

Dane had come to the crossroads of this conversation. She now had to choose which way she would go. She decided to keep her admiring listener rather than make the necessary concessions to pride in order to win a confidante.

"John and I have a difficult marriage," she said, enjoying the ambiguity of this statement. Polly began nodding animatedly. "Difficult, I mean, in the sense of challenging. With us, everything is, perpetually in growth. It's exhausting for me at times. We are always just a bit beyond where I can grasp. But it's a rewarding kind of exhaustion. Do you know what I mean?"

"No, but go on. It's fascinating."

"Well, it's as if . . . our marriage were a marriage of the future. It takes us further in awareness than either of us could go alone. Our marriage is a sort of spaceship." Dane sipped her drink. The banks of flowers around her seemed to hum a soft chorus for her tale. She felt like a poetess enchanting her audience from this hilltop above the sea.

"Wow. Let me tell you how I met my

131

husband. For a bit of comic relief. As I said, Karl wasn't my first husband. His name was Randall. This is the story of how I met Karl: he screwed me by mistake, in the dark. He thought I was his girl."

"Really?"

"Yes, really. See, as I said, Randall was in the Army. We were stationed in Germany—oh, this was five years ago—and came down here to Cala d'Or for a vacation. Randall, being gregarious Randall, was in with the local jet set —all two of them: Karl and his rich friend Jan—within a week. We all decided to have an evening picnic at the old fort—look, you can see it from here." She pointed out the same little ocher fort that Dane and John could see from their balcony. "We went out early one evening, on two of those little rafts you pedal. We took lots of food and wine and everybody got loaded. It was awfully hot and there was a full moon. Somebody suggested that we spend the night. So we all settled drunkenly into the moonlit ruins and, one by one, people dropped off to sleep. Randall began to snore peacefully. I was just lying there, mulling over the fact that I wasn't very happy with Randall, when suddenly a man climbed on top of me and began to pull down my shorts. I should now say that I screamed or wanted to scream or something, but it was really never even a possibility. It was like being visited by a nice incubus just when you needed one most. I had never been so excited in my life. To make a long story short, the dawn came and Karl woke up and found himself sleeping in my arms. He went all white and began apologizing. 'Why are you apologizing?' I said. 'I'm glad it happened.' He looked over his shoulder and there was his voluptuous girl friend—the one he *meant* to get—sleeping soundly not a yard from us. Then he looked at me for a while and started to grin. We would have started all over again if it hadn't been for the damn sun coming up. So we got up and went for a walk outside the ruins around the little island. Of course, I went back to Germany with Randall. I thought about Karl and regretted I'd married someone who'd never make me feel like Karl did. But I just accepted it. I never had any big ideals about marriage, really. Then Karl got my address and started writing. He was back in Amsterdam. We started meeting. Then, one day, he said, 'You know what you should do, don't you?' 'Come back to Amsterdam with you,' I said. So it was settled. We lived together till the divorce came through. Damn military crap. I beat the twins to the altar by six weeks. Well, dear, that's my contribution to this afternoon's story hour. Karl and I don't exactly have a marriage of the future. We have a rather primitive marriage, I'm afraid, based almost totally on sex. Is that awful?"

"Nothing's awful, as long as it works," Dane replied. The other girl's eyes glittered and danced, looking for something in her own. Was Polly teasing her in some way?

"It works so good I've gone and got myself pregnant again," said Polly. "I don't know what comes over me. I actually enjoy it more when I feel there's a chance of getting caught. Does that sound nuts?"

" 'Come and catch me, Mister Cosmos; I'll pay the bill later,' " Dane said. "You want to be swept away by something bigger than yourself." Yes, she understood that. Maybe Polly would come to visit in London. They would go to matinees together and flirt with confidences, always just skirting any admission which might give one of them the edge over the other.

"You see everything! God, am I glad you came. Look, you can't tell yet, can you?" She pressed her fingertips into her taut stomach beneath the black swimsuit.

"Not yet," Dane said.

"Look at them." Polly nodded toward the naked twins, who played in their sandbox some distance away, cheeping softly to each other, like little chipmunks. "The little dears ravaged me. I was in labor twenty-eight hours. I had to have nine stitches. One for every month. I gained two inches around the hips which I can never lose. My hipbones are permanently wider. How about you? Was your labor difficult?"

Dane thought she was having a joke at her expense. Then she remembered that, of course, the girl didn't know. "No. Everything went pretty smoothly for me."

"Everything goes pretty smoothly for you, doesn't it? Hey, you're not getting up to *go*, are you?"

"I've been gone since before lunch. They'll be worried about me," Dane said. The morning seemed to have been yesterday morning, some-how.

"Will you come back again?" asked Polly wistfully. She wrapped one bare foot around a leg and stood balanced like a lonely crane. "Wait—why not bring your family to lunch tomorrow! I can meet your wonderful husband and your little boy and Karl will make up a batch of his famous sangria."

"Well—actually we have a girl with us, too. A sort of patient of my husband's."

"Bring her along. Is she pretty? Karl will have someone to flirt with. I've decided that you have to come. No excuses. I'll show you a neat little shortcut to your hotel if you'll promise to come."

Dane laughed. Polly looked like a child with her freckles and the cropped black hair. Like a little gypsy who's begging you to love it. "I'm sure it will be okay. John would proba-bly like it," she said.

"Then that's settled. Actually, I've been having these same dreams, over and over again. I need somebody to tell me what they mean."

"He can, possibly."

Polly went with her through a cluster of pines, going slightly ahead like an Indian guide. Suddenly there was a clearing and hundreds of little stone steps leading down to the hotel's beach. "We're on the other side of the cove," explained Polly. "I'll bet you didn't realize you walked in a circle this afternoon, did you?"

Dane said good-bye, and went quickly down the stairs. The wind came up in her face

135

and she felt invigorated. Lively Polly Heykoop —that was a lucky find. You had to be a little on your guard with her; she said herself she was a connoisseur of other people's hangups. But if you were careful not to give anything away, it could be interesting. At least she had some sharpness to her. Poor Penelope. She supposed John could take her for a walk, break the news about Karl. Poor old Penelope, open and alone, vulnerable to the first woman-chaser she meets. Dane drew her own security around her like a cloak. Her own life did all right in the telling.

She spotted John and Robin on the beach. They were just on their way to the water's edge. Robin had on his swimsuit, but John was still in trousers and a shirt. He had, however, made the small concession to a holiday afternoon by taking off his shoes.

"Hello!" she called, hurrying across the beach. Several sunbathers watched. Neither John nor Robin looked especially pleased to see her.

"What's the matter?" she said when she reached them. "Why are you two looking like fussbudgets? I've had a wonderful afternoon." She told them about Polly and the twins. "And there's a nifty little problem with Penelope, John, that I suppose you can take care of in your inimitable way."

"I was worried about you," he said. "You might have said you were going off. If I weren't used to your utter disregard by now, I might have embarrassed us both by calling the police or some such thing."

"Oh God. Are you going to start being morbid?"

"Not to worry. You see, I worked out something about you while Robin was having his nap. You need a center from which to rebel. You try to see how far out you can go and still be taken back." He seemed quite pleased with his information.

She looked from one to the other of them. When Robin scowled, he had the wrinkles and pouches of an old man. John's fallen arch was visible beneath his trouser leg. The pale, misshapen foot, how alien it looked, curled into the healthy sand! This was her marriage of the future, her singular child who had given her not a single labor pain.

"Where's Penelope?" she asked.

"Out somewhere with her new beau, I should imagine."

"Beau! Ha. She has a surprise in store for her. I'm not the only one. Excuse me, I'm going upstairs."

"What surprise?" John said. "What are you talking about?"

"Oh, just a weird coincidence. Don't worry. I'll tell you later, when you come up."

"I'm coming now."

"But you only just came down. Doesn't he expect to go in the water?"

"We can come back," he said, following along beside her. Robin dragged back; he didn't want to leave the water.

"Oh, don't be so . . . urgent," she said, annoyed. "Why don't you two stay where you were?"

As their little trio ascended to the room, she said bitterly, "I don't know who's the worse, you or me, about having to know. If all else fails, that shared vice will probably cement us together for all time."

Chapter
Eight

After she had put Robin to bed, Dane went downstairs to sit on the terrace. She claimed a table in the corner, where there was a direct view across the little beach and up the steps that led toward Polly's villa. She ordered a Pernod even though she hated the taste and sat there quite peacefully sipping the licorice-like concoction and looking through the heavy mauve dusk at some distant lights beyond a black knot of trees. Those were the only lights on the hill and so must come from the Heykoops'. She pretended she had winged herself invisibly across the space between and hovered unseen over their conversation. Perhaps at this very minute they were discussing her. ("It was so strange. I had just finished spanking the twins when suddenly I heard this clapping coming from the road. I looked up and there she was. I knew instantly that we were going to be friends. She's invited me to stay with them in London. Her husband is a psychiatrist. I've asked them to lunch tomorrow. There's some girl coming with them, so you can flirt." And smooth Karl, what would he say? "Yes, I met that woman at the riding ring. She has a strange little boy. And that girl with them, she's a sweet little thing. Not bad on a horse.")

John and Penelope were walking along one or another of the village roads now. It had been agreed that he should explain casually that Dane had met Karl's wife and be supportive if Penelope had a setback. ("I want you to remember, Penelope, that you continue to have us in whatever capacity you choose to use us: friends, confidants, advisers, props. Holiday relationships can be suspended in a sort of void outside the frameworks of both parties because of the limited time, but . . .") Dane placed them on a deserted road, darkened by heavy pines. The same star she herself now saw from her table she placed in Penelope's line of teary vision as well. The girl would weep, quietly, for the destruction of an illusion, as she focused on the lone star shining through a nick in the pine branches.

This was fun, almost like God. Her terrace table was the hub of the universe as her mind swept over the doings of others. Perhaps all our activities, inconsistent and unpredictable things that they are, she thought, amused, are only the experimental branchings out of God's imagination as he sits bored at his table in the sky, sipping his Pernod. She wandered on to Robin, who was at this moment lying with open eyes in his cot, staring through the dusk-colored room, thinking . . . what? He was more difficult to "do." What had she thought about at age three? That period of her life, most of her early childhood, in fact, was blanked by a sort of amnesia. And besides, she had the feeling old Robin's thoughts were unique, totally his own and unmeasurable by any other child's. Damn that brat; he tore at her guts. Among all her people, the possessor of that cool little face, so closed against her, had the power to set her viscera writhing like worms in torment.

"Good evening, Mrs. Empson. I was walking along the shore and I found this. I thought your little boy might enjoy it." Mrs. Hart, dressed in a silk print whose flowers defied the dusk, stood beside Dane's table. She held out a soiled tennis ball.

"Oh, please sit down, Mrs. Hart," Dane said. "Thank you. I didn't bring one for him." She took the ball and slipped it into her purse.

"Well, perhaps I can stay just for a bit," said the lady, visibly pleased. "Then I must go and write letters to both my sons and their wives and send postcards to the children. I have five grandchildren. How did your little boy enjoy the horses today?"

"The Count—Bartolomé—said he was a born rider. This was his first time on a horse."

"Oh, you can't get them up too soon, Mrs. Empson. It comes naturally to them, before there's fear, you see. Little people have no conception of all the dangers we associate with large animals. Therefore, they learn quickly and it stays with them for the rest of their lives."

"Perhaps that's why I couldn't learn. I

was twelve when I had my first lesson. By then my mind was ticking over with all the possibilities of falls and injuries." Dane wondered how she would have turned out if someone like Mrs. Hart had been her mother. "You really understand children," she said. "I wish I did."

"Bless you, dear. That is true, I suppose. But you see, I happen to be one of those fossils people call a 'born mother.' It's what I've always wanted to be, since I was a very small girl. It's what I imagined myself being, just as, perhaps, you imagined yourself growing up to be an actress, or an artist."

"How interesting . . ." What had she imagined herself being as a child? She had contained a sort of future image, but it never took the form of any profession exactly. It had been more a matter of holding onto what she had, refining it. Her destiny was to be the result of her becoming supremely herself, with as few concessions as possible.

"Not always *interesting*," the other went on, pressing toward an honest definition. "Not always even pleasant. But what I wanted. Even in the dark moments, I never lost sight of that. For ever such a long time, I had given up hope."

"How do you mean?"

The old lady laughed. "Well, my dear, when I reached marriageable age, it was nineteen fifteen. There was hardly anybody around to marry. They were all being shot to pieces across the Channel."

"So what did you do, then?"

"I did the only thing one can do. I did what there was to be done. I had an invalid aunt, my mother's sister. She was married to an archaeologist and they were about to go out to Egypt. It was one of those painful situations where both of them knew she probably would not survive, but he didn't want to leave her behind and he had to go. They asked me to go with them to Cairo, to take care of her. Poor thing died aboard ship, on the way out. They buried her at sea. So there was I, with my uncle-in-law, who was twenty-five years older, and there was no turning back the ship."

"So you married him," said Dane.

"Not quite so simple as all that, my dear. You see, at the start I wasn't all that fond of him, really. I mean, I was twenty-three at the time and he was almost fifty! He was very taciturn, rather dour, as most Yorkshiremen are, and involved in his work. What emotions he did have had been beaten down during the slow death of my aunt. No, Geoffrey was not the man a young girl dreams of winning. For a long while, I never even considered the vague possibility. Oh, I felt sorry for this rather gruff old widower. And I felt a sort of family loyalty. He was kind to me, and, I think, felt a bit sorry for me, too. After all, I'd packed up my youth and sailed to Egypt with them. He said he'd like for me to keep his house in Cairo, live there, manage the servants, since he was to be away on digs most of the time. So I did, for five years. It wasn't at all an unhappy time because first of all I was very busy and then, too, I'd resigned myself to my lot and was grateful for what I had. When Geoffrey began showing little signs of affection, I was quite shocked at first. I pretended I was imagining them. Then he came right out and proposed. I was so upset, my dear. I told him I should have to go back to England, because I didn't think I could ever accept him and it wouldn't be fair to go on as we were with him feeling the way he did. And go back I did. I booked the first ship I could get and away I went, weeping my eyes out. Because it had been a good life, you see. Only I wasn't *in love*. But Geoffrey was a clever old thing. He knew me better than I knew myself. 'Of course, I'll miss you, my dear,' he said, 'but you must do what you feel you must. I would like to ask one favor, however. . . .' Oh, how well he knew what he was about! He asked me to go to Harrods, you see, and buy things for his house. He had always admired my taste, he said, and had I consented to marry him, he had planned to send me back to buy furnishing anyway. Well, I arrived back in England on my twenty-ninth birthday. I felt older than I am now. Everything had changed drastically since the war —places, people, styles of living. Duly, I went along to Harrods and began selecting things as I'd promised. And while I was debating about a certain curtain material—a lovely turquoise brocade; I'll never forget it—I suddenly thought: But this is all wrong; he'll *never* know how to order these made up. *And I'll never see how they turned out.* It was at this point that the decision was made, I think. Though, afterward, on the way back to Egypt, I justified my choice. It was so much better than total waste: Geoffrey being lonely in Egypt, having depended on me for years; and my going on hoping for something that might never have happened, back in England. If I ever had any doubts, they vanished when my first son, Charles, was born. That was *real*. I felt as if my whole life had led up to it. I remember there was another Englishwoman in the hospital who could not nurse her child. The doctor asked me if I would nurse her little one, temporarily. "You have so much, Mrs. Hart," he said. I remember thinking: Yes! I do have so much. So I nursed the woman's baby as well."

"How wonderful," said Dane, repelled by the image of a woman turned complacent dairy machine. "Did you get the material?"

"What material, dear?"

"The turquoise brocade, for the curtains."

"Oh, that material!" The old lady laughed aloud. Dane saw John coming across the terrace to them. "Yes, I got it, all right. I made the curtains myself. I remember the morning I hung them; I was in my second month of pregnancy."

"I'm glad you got them. Here comes my husband."

"Hello there," he said. "May I sit down, too?" He drew up a chair. "Nice to see you, Mrs. Hart. Have you two been having a chat?"

"Want a drink?" Dane asked him.

145

"No, thank you."

"I've been bending your wife's ear, Doctor."

"No, it was fascinating," said Dane. "I love to hear about other people's lives."

"Oh, tell me, too," said John.

"It was just women's talk, Doctor Empson." The old lady laughed. "Nothing as fascinating as all that. I'm sure the things *you* hear in your consulting room are much more interesting." Dane felt grateful to Mrs. Hart. Toctoc . . . a Ping-Pong game began behind them.

"How is Penelope?" Dane asked John. She propped her elbow on the table and laid her cheek in the cup of her palm. Suddenly she was so tired.

"She's all right. She went to her room to wash her hair."

"When a woman washes her hair, she's still among the living," Dane murmured dully.

"Mrs. Empson, are you feeling all right? I'm afraid my life story has overtired you."

"No, I loved it," Dane said, and then to John, "I think I'll go up to the room now. I *am* tired."

John frowned. He clearly did not want to go. Mrs. Hart was watching them both.

"You know"—Dane put her hand on the old woman's arm and got up—"I am exactly at your stage, when you were hanging those curtains, and I get tired much earlier."

Mrs. Hart went radiant. Now she understood everything! "My dear! How wonderful for you. Immediately, off to bed with you. I must go and do my letters." She rose, too, leaving John no choice but to follow suit. "You must let me know if I can do anything, if I can *tell* you anything." She winked knowingly and pinched Dane's arm affectionately.

As they left the terrace, Dane saw it was Mr. von Schirmbeck at the Ping-Pong table. He hopped lightly about, whacking the ball at his opponent, a beefy red-faced man. His face gleamed red and yellow and blue as he moved, its sweaty surface reflecting the colored lights strung around the trees. He lunged, grinning, at a high-flying ball and sent it *wham!* across the net. It grazed the table and lodged squarely in his opponent's crotch. The German contingent went wild with laughter. Dane giggled and Mr. von Schirmbeck smiled and nodded, rather boyishly shame-faced that she had seen.

"Why the sudden exit?" John asked in the room. "I was in the mood to stay and talk. What was that about curtains?"

"I really was tired, that was all. Oh, Mrs. Hart was hanging some curtains when she was two months pregnant. I suddenly had the urge to tell somebody I was pregnant, just for the hell of it, and see how it would feel."

"Well, how did it feel?"

"No special way. Maybe it would have if I *had* been. I think it made her like me better, that was all. I can't understand all this fuss about motherhood. Maybe something has been left out of me. Is Penelope in despair?"

"Not at all. She took it rather calmly. She was a bit piqued at first. As much by my telling her as by the Dutchman's neglecting to tell her, I think. But that's all right. I can handle that."

"She should be damned grateful that we look out for her interests," Dane said, peeved at the girl. "I suppose she was making wedding plans and blames us for taking away her dream."

"No, she said she was happy to have what she has with him. I don't know what that is; I didn't think it was an appropriate time to ask. She said he has made her feel alive again and she is grateful for that."

"Oh, all this making-do," said Dane. She went to touch Robin's sleeping face, translucent under the glow of the bedside lamp. She fussed with his covers. He looked exactly like a small divinity, utterly untouchable. "Why does nobody dare to say, 'I want it all'?"

"I dare to say it," John replied quietly. "And so do you."

Struck by something in his voice, she looked up and saw him newly, in his own space again. There were the fierce ambivalent features lit by the lamp at Lady Jane's; crackling in the depths of his brown eyes were those intimations of a yet uncoded soul. It was as if she had returned to that first evening, as if she sat once again at his feet, wondering how she could get him, at the same time basking in the foreknowledge that this strange brilliance was none other than her husband. She stood, hardly breathing, holding this vision of his face, balancing the two perspectives, finding her love for him in this no-man's-land between the two moments in time.

"Go and have your bath," he said, in a rare moment of keeping his distance, and all the way to the bathroom she walked as though treading air, fearful of thudding back to earth, fearful of breaking the exquisite tension. On the threshold, she turned quickly, perversely, hoping to catch him watching her with the old moist look. But he was on his way to the balcony.

My story is by far the best, she thought, brushing her teeth with an agreeably gum-stinging toothpaste, thinking of the man on the balcony, dark head framed by galaxies of stars. (Why had he been able to leave her so quickly?) Face it: breakdowns in Fortnum's followed by a foxy philanderer's attentions; or being screwed by mistake in the moonlight ruins of an old fort which leads no farther than the laundromats of Amsterdam; or taking old Geoffrey via blue brocade in order to swell into one's lifetime ambition of being *magna mater* ("You have so much . . .")—all nice stories to listen to, but I wouldn't want to live there. (Why had he rushed out there? To think some new thought? "And hid his face amid a crowd of stars . . .") "John and I have a difficult marriage. Difficult, I mean, in the sense of challenging. . . . Our marriage is a sort of spaceship."

She bared clean, square teeth at herself in the mirror, brushed her hair and went to the balcony.

"You look like some gloomy Gothic hero posed against the battlements," she said to his back. The stars were all over the sky. "What are you thinking?" She came up beside him and slipped an arm about his waist.

"About negative and positive responses —this idea I've been developing. It seems to me one could arrange them in a scale, only—" He pressed her arm absently with his elbow and continued to look out to sea, toward the fort. "I haven't quite worked it out yet."

"Does it have anything to do with . . . us?"

He laughed softly and put his arm about her. "No, not this one. Except, of course, for the fact that we're humans and it's a kind of chart of human responses. Otherwise it's not to do with you, or with us, directly. You like that and you don't like it, hmm?"

"Oh, John. You know me so well. It's terrible." She snuggled closer.

"It's not terrible. I know you and I want to know more; you're afraid if you give yourself away there'll be none left. I'm telling you it's limitless. We are limitless."

"I was thinking in the bathroom how really lucky I am. It's just that I'm blind to it nine-tenths of the time. Why? We have all it takes to make this into something really special. I told Polly Heykoop our marriage was like a spaceship. She thought I was lucky as as hell."

"I'm looking forward to meeting her. And Karl, too. It's interesting, the patterns people make."

"So interesting! John, listen, quick before I lose it: everything seems boundless, right now, like all these stars. I feel we're standing in the middle of a limitless universe and it's all ours to explore. I see how we can be, together. Don't let me lose us, through my own perversity. If you could hold us on course, just a little longer, until I'm able to help."

"I try, darling. I still believe in this thing. I don't think you're an Angela. . . . Did I tell you about Angela, my childhood friend?"

"No, tell me now." She pushed close to him, trying to blot herself out.

"Well, when I was six—we were living in South Africa then—Angela was the little girl next door. We became best friends. I decided we could build an airplane and fly away in it together. She was very excited about the idea. So I began. I went about it very methodically, designing it from a science book. I made it out of packing cases. The wings were several yards long. The propeller was to be driven by a steam engine I'd built with a can of water and a fire to be lit underneath, when the time came. The jet of steam would impinge on a sort of paddle wheel. It took me weeks and weeks of work. Angela stayed by my side, interested throughout. Eventually, all was ready for the maiden voyage. We sat in it, ready for flight. I lit a fire under the can of water. This took a while, because it was windy, but eventually it caught and I became excited. At this point, Angela grabbed the can of water and poured it over the fire. 'I got scared,' she said and began to cry. I realized that what had been a real project to me was only an insulated dream for her."

"What happened after that?"

"It was all spoiled. Of course, I tried again later, alone. But nothing happened. For a long time after, I believed that the first attempt would have succeeded whereas the others didn't, and I couldn't forgive her for botching it."

"Brrr. That story gives me the creeps," Dane said.

"'The road not taken,'" quoted John, "should give anyone the creeps."

Dane imagined the Mrs. Hart who might have been, had she stuck up for her ideals, braved London at twenty-nine: Mrs. Something Better—or perhaps supremely herself. "Oh God, I don't want to be ordinary," she said.

"To be that, you would have to cripple yourself," he replied.

"Then you haven't given up on me yet?"

"No. Whatever possibilities for good there are in our marriage won't be killed by me."

"Let's sleep out here on the balcony, John."

"Yes, all right." He turned to her, letting his pleasure flood into her space. Damn it. Why couldn't he keep up the balancing act? The distant, stately lover floated away, far away as the cold stars, which seemed to laugh softly at her impossible romanticism. "Wait here, I'll go fetch the mattresses," he said. He knew she was having trouble preserving it.

When he disappeared into the room, she began to undress. She would go through with it anyway as a sort of gesture toward their marriage of the future. She would not pour water on the little flame. Who could tell? Maybe they *would* fly away this time. She tried to retain the resurgence of feeling she'd had for him back in the room when he'd been walking away. *Stranger in the armchair. Craggy Gothic husband.* She dropped her bra to the stone floor. Down below, the ocean lapped, licking gently at the corners of the little beach.

"Darling?" John touched her on the shoulder. He was naked. She leaned over the balcony wall, not looking at him. Not yet. If she could just stand close to the other body, seeking it slowly in her own time, finding the contours of its alienness. He waited. Sooner than she would have liked, she traced an arc across his moon-blue skin. If only he were pure stranger! What would it be like to make love with an angel? Cool, pure, remote. As impersonal as the face of that little child who slept so autonomously in the next room.

"I want to be closer to you," John said. He had put the mattresses together and spread a soft blanket over them. She lay down beside him.

An angel would not need anything. He would simply lay himself out for her, let her crucify him with her body, his face frosted with magnificent disinterest, just a touch of a smile.

John knelt above her. "Are you warm enough?"

"Yes."

They were at the fort. Randall was snoring. Suddenly, the body of the strange doctor loomed above her. Darkly, he set about his business. Welcome the incubus. Not a sound was uttered.

"Dane."

They are at the fort. John is asleep beside her. Suddenly, the stranger covers her with his body. It is Karl, who has mistaken her for another. She lets him persist in his mistake.

Why is it always so dry? John, so tentative, apologetic. "Is it all right for you?"

For days she and the driver have been traveling on an empty bus, hurtling between anonymous, dusty countries. They flirt through his rear-view mirror. He is nameless and coarse. She has no say-so in the matter of his stopping the bus. Finally, in the dead of night, he hurries her into a third-rate hotel. The woman behind the desk grins and hands over a key. Not a word is said. In the room, he tears off her clothes, slaps her twice across the face and knocks her down on the bed. Makes her lie with her legs open and beg for him. Teases her. Laughs at her. Makes her take it in her mouth.

Can no degradation take her where she wants to go?

Taciturn and determined to procreate, the old man is seeking her. Geoffrey presses relentlessly for his conjugal rights. ("I shall make a milk machine of you, my dear....")

Soon, now, perhaps.

("In a moment, all will be lost. It will be

too late. The process will have been started. Your breasts will begin to swell with milk enough to suckle the hungry mouths of the entire world. They will drag the ground. In one minute I am going to transform you into a universal teat. Are you ready? Sixty, fifty-nine, fifty-eight . . .") He tosses his whip, his features darken into Moorish ones. ("Are you ready, filly?") He beats her. The lashes sting her sunburned skin. Sharp whelks, flame red, flare across her breasts and belly. Faster and faster he beats. ("Lie down in the straw, filly.") In half a minute it will all be too late, you will swell beyond recognition. ("Now I tell you what you are going to do my angel. You will let Pepe, Antonio, Bernardo, Ricardo, José and Juan—all the hired hands on the island—ride you. Ready, Pepe? Saddle her. Just a few seconds for each of you. There are so many waiting to ride. She is my prize. There, that was a nice quick one! Now the next one. Spread her a little and maybe Bernardo and Ricardo can ride together and save time. Three of you want to ride? All at once? Is impossible! No? Okay, we can try. José, you slip in there; Pepe, over there; Tonio, good. Now all together: stay in the saddle! Riiiide!") She is split down the middle and overflowing. Cries out.

And John accepts it.

Beyond their poor fallible act, the stars blinked on, in brittle silvery amusement. She lay under him, allowing a decent interval to elapse. At one point she said, "What if you and Angela had caught on fire?"

"Mmmh? What, sweet?" He was almost

asleep. She rolled him over and slid off the mattress and went in to the bathroom. Excellent Spanish conveniences. Funny how these things were made in England, then exported, quick-quick, to the hot-blooded sensual countries. She sat for a while, letting the warm water gush inside her, cleansing and purifying her.

They had been married at Chelsea Registry Office in June and driven to Sandwich for the weekend. Between London and their destination, a traffic jam ensnarled them. Crawling along in their rented Humber, they discussed the limitations of the others present at their marriage ceremony. Dane had asked the editor of the magazine to be her witness. A smart, expedient divorcée in her forties, she arrived punctually in her Chanel suit, its jacket weighted with chains, darted curious looks at John while the official was singsonging the ceremony, and left immediately after, hailing her own taxi from the curb.

"I don't think she approved of you," giggled Dane. "I don't think there was any room in her value system for an odd bird like you. You don't wear the latest fashions, drive a Jaguar or make clever chitchat. Why *did* I marry you? Hell, you don't even have a title."

John laughed. "Peter Lewis was equally dubious of you."

Peter Lewis was John's old classmate from Oxford, a silent, plump mathematician. He and John had not seen each other for at least ten years, but he dutifully subjected himself to the morning "milk train" from Oxford, where he wae now a don, in order to stand up for a friend. He also left immediately after the ceremony, bumbling some excuse about an old aunt just this side of Chiswick.

"I'm sure Peter expected me to come up with someone more solid. Not that you aren't. You're solid as a rock in terms of being you. But your appearance belies your solidity."

"How? How does it?" She liked this sort of discussion.

"You sort of glitter rather than glow. Small talk comes easy to you. You dress well. You are all crisp, sharp edges. You look like one of those young career women on the go."

This description did not displease her. "Flash-in-the-pan American girl nets obscure English genius," she said. Who cared about pleasing the plump Peter Lewises.

"That sound like a headline from your magazine."

They decided they were glad neither parent had come. Mrs. Empson had sent a civil perfumed note from the Isle of Man with a fifty-pound check stapled to it. Her church would not permit her to attend, she wrote. She hoped they would be happy. Dane's father taught at the War College during summer. ("Why can't you wait?" he had asked in the brief transatlantic call. "If it's good now, it will be good in three months.") They could not wait, Dane explained, because it had been decided. His reasoning made good sense, but something beyond reason urged her to get the thing done, to make it irrevocable as soon as possible.

"Why is it so few people can see beyond contingencies?" she said.

They reached their hotel, on the edge of a rather sinister-looking waterway, at dusk. The water looked black. The proprietress apologized for the freak onslaught of mosquitoes. They ate unexciting English food in the dining room. Dane asked if they could have white wine to go with the plaice, which arrived almost cold. But the waiter brought red, explaining they were out of white.

After dinner they went for a walk. The houses leaned slightly forward over the narrow cobbled streets. Very few people were about; one or two, hurrying in and out of a shop, crossing a street. It was as though they had the little town to themselves. They went through a neat park full of brooding, heavy oaks. It was after nine, but the sky was a phosphorescent indigo. John held her hand as they walked. This is my husband now, she thought, looking sidewise at his profile and preserving its strangeness in her heart. He began to recite a poem she had never heard in a deep and sorrowful voice:

> "Very old are the woods
> And the buds that break
> Out of the briar's boughs,
> When March winds wake,
> So old with their beauty are—
> Oh, no man knows
> Through what wild centuries
> Roves back the rose."

Just before he had come to bed, looking at her with the soft brown eyes before turning off the light, she had been afraid. What if it wasn't any good on their wedding night? He embraced her in the dark room. She could hear the slow, torpid movement of the black waterway outside. Such a dank, lonely little place. Those dark oaks. She summoned back the interesting stranger in the armchair at Lady Jane's, taped in the deep and sorrowful voice reciting: "So old with their beauty are—/Oh, no man knows/ . . ." and sumperimposed upon this image the statement: This is my husband, I now belong to this man. She worked hard. Through her own resources, she was not cheated of her bride's fulfillment.

" 'Oh, no man knows/Through what wild centuries/Roves back the rose,' " she whispered, crouched over the bidet in the dark bathroom. The poem was still the beauty and the mystery it had been the first time she heard it. *That* had not diminished through familiarity. Ah, but that was because *no man knows.* She dried herself, slipped into a nightgown and went into the bedroom to see about the child. John had turned off the little bedside lamp and she knelt beside the cot and listened for his breathing. At first she could not hear it. She put her face close to his mouth. Yes, there it was: the sweet, regular breath, soft as down. Then she looked into wide, staring blue eyes. *How* could a child sleep with its eyes open? It baffled her. She passed her hand back and forth in front of the eyes. Not a blink. Could he see her?

Did his vision register her form even in his unconsciousness? She would like to ask Mrs. Hart these things, but knew she would not. She continued to kneel there, above him, pondering the eyes. Down below, the ocean continued its gentle assault on the little beach. Outside on their balcony, John slept the sound sleep of consummation. When she got tired of kneeling, she sat down on the cool floor and went on looking at the child. Those wide staring eyes comforted her. What did they see? What vigil were they keeping? They stared back at the night, protecting her from chaos as well.

Chapter
Nine

Robin screamed. His small naked body was strung tight with rage. He screamed again and went red all the way down to his bare feet, which danced madly on the tile floor. At each new scream, Dane expected him to shatter apart.

"Robin," said John firmly, "that will do you no good. Do you hear? The sooner you put on your clothes, the sooner we can all go down and eat breakfast."

John had been up before sunrise, dressed and full of energy. He had taken their mattresses back inside and helped Dane stagger to bed in the cool room before the sun had a chance to touch the balcony. She had dozed, peaceful in the knowledge of having pleased John to the point where he could go away from her for a while. She had heard his pen scratch-scratching away, sheets of foolscap being flipped over rapidly, as he wrote in the dawn light of the balcony. Around eight-thirty, she had got up, feeling refreshed, and gone to pull Robin out of bed and begin the arduous task of dressing him, a task she had often complained to John about. But this morning, just as she had knelt to help Robin with his pants, John had appeared in the doorway. "We are going to let Robin dress himself this morning," he said. "He does at Mrs. Christopher's, you know. We've been spoiling him. I've worked out quite a lot of things this morning, and that's one of them. I've decided this holiday is going to work." Dane had liked the sternness that came into his eyes. At last, John had taken over the task of steering their lives. If lovemaking had given him this new firmness, then it was a small price to pay. But Robin had been screaming at them for fifteen minutes now, and had not touched his clothes, and Dane was beginning to doubt the efficacy of these sudden new controls.

"Look, I'm getting hungry," she said, in the space between two screams. "Has it occurred to you this little war could go on all day?"

"It won't." John went dark. "Robin, stop screaming and listen to me. Do you want your breakfast? A glass of milk and one of those nice sweet buns that you like?"

The child nodded and began to wail anew.

"Well, put on your socks, then."

Robin let out a terrible shriek.

"Damn it, John, the maids are outside. Everybody can hear him."

"Let them. That's how children dominate people who care about appearances. Robin, if you want to eat, you'd better put on that sock. Just pick it up, sit down on the floor and put your toes in. No, Mommy's not going to do it for you."

Forty-five minutes later, a more or less clothed child stood before them. His face was lumpy and swollen from crying. His shirt was on backward. One sock, stretched and damp, disappeared into the heel of his shoe. Dane lay across her bed, totally depleted, hating the look of triumph on John's face.

"Well," he said, "what do you say we all go down to breakfast?"

"Can I at least turn his shirt around, and maybe comb his hair?"

"I'd rather you didn't. It would spoil our hour's work. I think he's going to come around now. Tomorrow morning it will be less of a trauma. Before we leave, he'll take pride in being able to do it. At breakfast, I have another idea I want to present to you."

"I hope it's not as exhausting as this one."

John went into their closet to get something. Her eyes met Robin's. Poor little thing looked so . . . diminished. She couldn't stand seeing him with his dignity torn away like this. A disciplined child, red face swollen and blotched from useless protest. Furtively, she took her own hairbrush and did his hair. She was just tugging the little sock out of the shoe when John's head emerged from the closet. "Darling, I wish you wouldn't destroy *all* our hard work."

Penelope was not waiting for them in the dining room. The waiter was just clearing away her coffee cup. Her napkin had been refolded neatly beside a plate bearing traces of butter and *ensaimaida* crumbs.

"Hmm. Well, she seems to have kept her appetite," Dane said. "Where's she gone off to, in such a hurry? She always waits for us in the morning, to tell us what she dreamed."

"She may be feeling a bit defenseless. That's natural. Like a child who goes out on his own for the first time and fails. He's ashamed to face his parents—and we *are*, in a sense, parent figures to her. It's understandable she might not feel comfortable with us, just at this point."

"I'll go by her room after breakfast and see what she's up to," Dane said. She saw herself knocking briskly at the girl's door, going in and lifting the whole thing to a tone of dry sarcasm against the world of ridiculous men. ("What do you expect, Penelope? They're all such children. Get all the experience you can from him; it will help you manipulate your future ones.")

"That would be nice. Let her know we're here for her. Don't treat her like Camille, though."

Robin ate his bun attentively. He swung his legs against the chair. Once or twice a funny little drone issues from his mouth.

"Listen, he's humming to himself," John said. "He's much happier, knowing what is expected of him. Would you like to hear the rest of my idea concerning our holiday?"

"What?" She dreaded it, a little.

"There is not a reason in the world why we shouldn't stay an extra week," he said, smiling. "We're not just the ordinary family on holiday, we're more complex. Therefore, if it takes *them* a week to unwind so that they can enjoy their other week, it seems logical that it might take a trio like us two weeks to unwind. To my mind, we only began our holiday last night. How does this seem to you?"

She said, "Penelope will have to get back for her job."

"That's all right. We can go down to Palma with her in the taxi, even do a bit of sightseeing after her plane goes. I spoke to Ramírez-Suárez. Our room won't be available after next week, but he has another one."

There was not any reason, really, why they shouldn't stay another week. But the very latitude depressed her. It gave one rope enough to hang oneself. She would rather, as the poem went, they had "promises to keep." It bothered her that it mattered so little to her whether they stayed or went. Penelope would be madly envious. The extra week put them in another category: that of people who did not have to meet a schedule to ensure their livelihood.

"What about your patients?" she asked.

"No one's urgent just now; I can send wires to the ones with appointments."

That gnawed at her, too. She would have liked her husband's patients to be urgent as all hell.

"Ramírez-Suárez agreed to show us the room at ten." He looked at his watch. "Why not run along and see Penelope? It's a quarter to, now. I'll wait for you in the lobby, with Robin."

Dane knocked at the girl's door. No answer. She put her ear to it. No sound. She opened it and went in. Penelope was not there. The bed had been made and several items of clothing lay neatly at the foot of it: skirt, blouse, panties and bra. She must have gone swimming, then. Dane wandered about, examining Penelope's style of living. She went into the bathroom. The girl had brought her own soap: expensive, scented little bars with carved flutings. A luffa, to rub up circulation, on the rim of the tub ... and in the medicine cabinet? Spray deodorant, mouthwash, eyedrops, Moon Drops, Brush 'n Blush, facial moisture balm, bath oil ("washes away dry skin"), dental floss, aspirin, Ovulen, Entero-Vioform ... The old girl had certainly come armed for battle, all right. She went back into the bedroom and examined the things on the bedside table. What was Penelope doing reading *The Brothers Karamazov*? The marker halfway through the book ... Improving her mind? Was she able to read this stuff after she found out Karl was a married man? Dane picked up a dark-blue leather-bound writing pad. She flicked it open. "Dear Mum and Dad, This is a ..." was written in a candid, girlish hand. This is a *what*? There was a plastic bottle of expensive body lotion. These working girls— lavishing their tiny salaries on creams and dreams. Dane uncapped the bottle and sniffed. Exotic. Lemon and wild lilies and ... something else. She rubbed a little on her wrist and sniffed again. Nice. She helped herself to a liberal portion, did her arms and neck and legs. That felt better. She recapped the bottle and frowned at the level. She hadn't used much. The nice thing about being single was coming back to your own lair at night. Take a bath with fragrant soap, slick yourself down with lotion and lie under clean cool sheets replenishing yourself, reordering and discarding the materials of your day. Anything, any*body* you didn't want, you left outside the door. Tomorrow a miracle might happen. Meanwhile, a few pages of *Karamazov* or Proust slurping his madeleine, just to feel you were civilized, then off to an uncluttered sleep. Penelope, in a way, was the lucky one: riding and walking and being flattered by the Dutchman, perhaps being seduced among wildflowers in the island woods, then back to lie in her own fragrances and dream of being married to the perfect Karl, while the real wife of the imperfect one ran herself frazzled after two devil twins and stayed home in the afternoons envying people like Dane. Dane noticed a little drawer in the bedside table and opened it, half expecting to find a diary. Only a few wadded Kleenexes. She left the room, vaguely dissatisfied.

"That was a nice long chat," said John. He and Robin and Ramírez-Suárez were waiting for her in the lobby.

"Oh. She wasn't there."

"What took you so long?"

"I was composing my soul."

"The room I show you are just up the road a little," said Ramírez-Suárez.

"Up the road?" asked Dane.

"Yes. In our *annex*." He pronounced the word proudly, as thought it were the latest thing in technology. "You see, I tell the doctor, the hotel is full up beginning next week. That is why you could not go ahead in your nice room with the balcony. But this is a nice accommodation also, in our annex. The family who have it will be leaving at the end of the week. The French people with the adorable little children. They have been very happy there."

"I'm sure we will be, too," John said, trying to take her hand as they followed the manager out into the hot sun. But she hurried ahead of him, alert to be admitted to the actual rooms of the woman who fascinated her.

The annex was a good two city blocks from the hotel. Unshaded by any trees, it looked more like a white-washed barracks, hurriedly constructed to house extra troops. There were no shrubs yet, or flowers. Some few blades of grass were trying hard to emerge from the red clayey soil. Ramírez-Suárez went around to a side entrance, knocked self-effacingly at a screen door, put his ear to the door. "Ah! Good, they are at the beach. I was just making sure," he said. "Will you please go in, Doctor? Señora?"

They went in. There were two small, very hot rooms, one leading into the other, with a little bathroom at the end. The entire area was smaller than their hotel bedroom. Red cotton curtains were drawn over the windows, giving the rooms a reddish glow and making them seem hotter. The little daybeds were pushed against the walls.

"It's awfully warm in here," she said, walking about in what little space there was. The room was impersonally neat. Everything must be put away in the closet.

"But the señora will be at the beach most of the day," ventured Ramírez-Suárez.

"That's true," seconded John.

She would have given anything to look in that closet. But not while the others were around. How did they live in this tiny space? Crowding and bumping into one another, the four of them? Did the Frehchman and his wife push those narrow daybeds together for making love? How did the woman ever get herself together? There was not even a mirror. She herself could survive, *just* survive, in their present accommodations. She would not last an hour in these.

"What's the bathroom like?" she murmured, just to appear fair. She had already rejected the possibility of the Empsons staying in these rooms. The French family might live here as they did in the eyes of the world: spontaneously, effortlessly, without reflection; the Empsons could not.

As she went ahead to the bathroom, Ramírez-Suárez said quietly to John, "And of course, these *two* rooms cost less than the price of your one."

"Oh dear, no tub," said Dane. "I'm afraid it's out. I have a skin condition," she explained to the manager, "which requires me to bathe twice a day in a special oil." John frowned at her, but he wouldn't betray her.

"I am sorry," said the manager. "The doctor did not mention—"

"My fault," put in John quickly. "Do you have any other rooms?"

"Oh, Doctor, is a miracle we have even these. Next week is the season starting. Everything else is booked for months ahead."

"I see," John said. "Well, perhaps my wife and I should think about this. Perhaps I could let you know later today."

"Later today. Certainly!" Ramírez-Suárez was eager to get out of this uncertain atmosphere.

Going back to the hotel, Dane said to Robin, "How would you like to go for a swim, kiddo?" The child nodded solemnly. "Well, come on, then!" She took his hand, which curled at once into hers. "Let's run, want to?"

She and the child broke into a trot, leaving John to walk behind with the manager. "Hurry, hurry!" she cried gaily, feeling freed from the extra week in those horrid little rooms.

There was just the beginning of a smile on Robin's face as he ran along beside her.

They went down to the beach *en famille*.

"I'm *not* going to let you wriggle out of that swim to the fort," said John, tacitly implying that she had wriggled out of the extra week.

"What do you hope to get by swimming out there?"

"It's something I see us doing together —a sort of token quest, I suppose."

"Oh. Well, why not? We have several more days left. Let's start earlier, though. There isn't time now. We're due at Polly's at one. She rang up and left a message. I think she was secretly afraid we wouldn't show up."

Penelope, deeply tanned, sat on her towel. She had just come out of the water and was replaiting her hair, which was a rich golden color.

"Well, Penelope, you're making yourself scarce today. I went by your room, but you weren't there. Has John told you we're invited for lunch?" Dane sat down beside the girl. John and his son walked down to the shallows.

"Mmm," said Penelope. She looked Dane straight in the eye. Her own eyes had become the same green as the sea. The blond lashes were still wet from swimming. "I swam a hundred and forty strokes in the sea and thought everything over and decided I wasn't going to give up so easily. Now I'm looking forward to it. Besides, I'm dying to know what she's like. Wouldn't you be, in my circumstances?"

Dane wasn't sure what Penelope's "circumstances" were exactly, but knowing Penelope, she would soon find out. "You mean Polly?"

"Yes. What is she like? John said you had quite a long visit yesterday. The whole thing is rather strange, isn't it? I can say that, now I've had my swim and made my resolutions. Last night I cried my eyes out and decided to avoid everyone. But there's only a few more days of holiday and, I decided today, I'd only be hurting myself. There'll be plenty of time for all that stoic nonsense when I'm back in London. No, I've made up my mind to make the most of it: Karl, even the dramatics of the situation, you coming upon his wife by chance —strange! Is she pretty?"

"Not pretty; she's—"

"Would you mind rubbing some oil on me, here?" She turned her shoulder. "I'm getting browned up for the kill."

"Sure." Dane poured some of the expensive stuff in her palm and began companionably rubbing the girl's shoulders and back with it. "Polly's got this sort of gypsy-like quality: dark, alive, alert—and also something cagey. Those shiny black eyes—wait till you see them—poking about in search of secrets."

"What *I* want to see is his face, when he sees me. Too bad—it would be even better if he had no way of knowing I was coming beforehand."

"Yes. If you were sprung on him out of the blue! As it is, he's had almost twenty-four hours to prepare a face to meet the faces that he meets."

Both girls laughed at this remark. Dane pretended to be Karl, in front of his shaving mirror. "Good after*noon*, Miss MacMahon, so glad you could come . . . No, no. Good afternoon, Penelope, so nice to see you again after our *ride* yesterday . . . No, no. Good afternoon, it is good to see you . . . that way giving away no more than necessary. Ya! Good afternoon, period. . . ."

From above them, John said, "I wonder,

172

Penelope, could you keep an eye on Robin while we swim?"

"Of course. Dane, you are terrible, terrible. But it helps. It puts things in perspective somehow."

"Shall we go in?" John asked Dane. "We have yet to swim together."

Dane left Robin and Penelope, who was still tittering at the impersonation of Karl, and walked dutifully beside John toward the sparkling sea.

"I thought we might try and swim, say, a third of the way to the fort," came his pleasant voice by her ear. "To get in training."

When they were knee-deep in water, Robin's first scream came. They looked back. There he was, in a red stiff rage, screaming after them. Penelope knelt beside him, being ineffectual. Like sleepers awakened, the beach population roused themselves, one by one, to stare at their favorite sideshow.

"One of us had better go back," Dane said.

"No. Let him scream. He has to learn we want to be by ourselves sometimes. Let's go on."

"I couldn't enjoy it now. We're the goddamn center of attention. I'm going back."

He caught her arm. He went very dark. "No, don't go back." The brown eyes tried to persuade her of the urgency of this request.

"All this fuss about going *swimming!*" She jerked her arm away. "Why is it the Empsons cannot do the simplest thing without some grand-scale emotional screw-up witnessed by the whole world? How can I swim now? It would be a chore, a conscious act of will, and no pleasure. I'm going back."

As she splashed out of the sea, she thought she heard John curse Robin.

"Sorry," said Penelope, looking flustered. "I couldn't do a thing with him."

"God, Robin, you are a bore." Dane sank to her knees on the towel and drew him to her. He only whimpered now. "Look, you've made me halfway wet and halfway dry." John was swimming laps determinedly. "Your little shoulders are red. Let me rub some stuff on them" She clasped the snuffling child between her knees and oiled the rigid little back with Penelope's fancy suntan lotion. "You don't mind, do you, Penelope?"

"Please. Use all you want."

As she rubbed him with long sensuous swipes, she put her nose into his fine hair and inhaled its damp fragrance.

"I want you to tell me the honest truth," said Penelope. "Do you think I should sleep with him? I know he's not in love with me, but I'm terribly attracted to him. I might regret not doing it, later. What would you do?"

"I," said Dane, "would probably not. Not unless he first offered to leave his wife and children. And then"—she laughed rather hysterically—"I probably wouldn't enjoy it. But I think you should. It will be beautiful for you. Something to give color and warmth to all your horrible, lonely winter months to come." She knew she should stop now but couldn't. "He, of course, will go back to Holland and

174

forget all about you, except for an occasional sweet tugging in the groin. He and Polly will go on having babies—she's pregnant again, did you know?—and maybe he'll even paint a picture of you, your nude body as he remembered it—"

"Stop it; you're being cruel," said the girl, looking about to cry.

"I'm not being cruel! I'm being the best friend you could have," Dane said with feeling. She stroked Robin's soft flesh and he let her. She was not sorry he had shrieked her back from that dutiful swim. "For Christ's sake, I'm telling you *you'll* have the best of the deal."

"I'm sorry, then. I don't understand you. It seems to me you're saying I'll have nothing."

"*You'll* have the Karl who is eternally fascinating to you." Dane crushed the stiff child to her. Now *she* was about to cry. Yet she was angry, with stupid Penelope, with everyone in the world.

"No I won't. What do you mean? Polly will have him."

Chapter
Ten

Karl Heykoop grasped Penelope by the shoulders and turned her toward the sun. "Do you see?" he said to his wife. "Didn't I tell you? It is *light* under there. Out of most people's pores comes a darkness."

"Are you saying the rest of us have blackheads?" Polly asked, winking at Dane and John. They had just arrived and were waiting for a proper acknowledgment after Karl finished assessing Penelope's skin. He has decided to play the appreciative artist, thought Dane. "Don't all blondes have a lightness under their skin?" asked Polly.

"Not at all," said Karl, rather censoriously. "It is not pigment I am talking about. It is . . . almost a spiritual quality."

"Oh, *I* see."

Dane felt the Heykoops were going through a little softshoe routine to provide their new guests with a quick sketch of how they worked their marriage. Look, darling, what do you think of the artistic possibilities of my new mistress?

Penelope stood in the middle of the terrace, flushing, letting herself be handled, perused like an object. John stood off to the side, a polite little smile on his face. He had slicked his hair with a wet comb, a thing she hated, and looked like a shy boy hoping to make a good impression at a party. Only Robin had any dignity. He took in the little charade with impassive blue eyes and remained himself. Dane put her hand on his neck, allying herself with him.

"What I am dying to do," said Karl, mostly to his wife, but including everyone, "is to paint her astride Serafina, á la Godiva, of course. Cannot you see all those golds?"

"You'd better ask the horse first," said Polly. "Won't you all sit down? Karl will get everyone some sangria, won't you, Karl? John, if I act shy around you, it's because I'm in awe of you. Dane said, among other things, that you were the most intelligent man in the world."

"That was nice of you, dear," John replied, and said nothing further. Dane wished he had made some obliquely clever comeback, denying her assertion and yet demonstrating its truth. This was going to be a very long afternoon.

Karl said to Penelope, "After lunch, maybe I do a few crayon sketches, just to get the lie of the land."

John had turned his back on them and was looking out toward the little fort.

"Can I help you get lunch together?" Dane asked Polly.

"No, but you can come and talk while I take it out of the refrigerator."

"Come on, Robin. Let's go explore Polly's kitchen." She was rather gratified at the way Robin was sticking to her. He had not forgiven his father for making him dress himself this morning. She hadn't, quite, herself. It had made him into just another child. And Robin's silent, wise-seeming aloofness was becoming important to her. She hadn't realized how much until she had seen it threatened. She didn't want him to be just a child.

As soon as they were in the kitchen, Polly said, "John isn't at *all* what I had expected.

Dane felt as if the girl had thrown a glass of cold water on her. "What do you mean?" she said, trying to sound casual.

Polly opened the refrigerator and took out potato salad, cold chicken, a lettuce and to-mato and cucumber salad, already dressed, a platter full of ham. She began slicing bread, holding the loaf against her stomach and cut-ting toward her unborn child. "He's really very sweet," she said. "And rather shy. I had pic-tured some dark giant who would tower over us all and make us feel ill at ease. As it is, I feel I want to make *him* feel at ease—not that he looks nervous or anything. It's like I feel I can say, 'Come and join our circle,' and he'll be willing and even pleased." She looked down at Robin. "That child's eyes! They frighten me. He seems to be looking right into my soul and sorting through all my black secrets. He looks like a little *man,* somehow. Do you think so? Does he ever talk?"

"Only to people he's been around. He talks to his—the woman who keeps him sometimes; he talks to John, they have little discussions; sometimes he comes out with amazing 'insights. And of course he talks to me."

"Of course!" Polly laughed. "You're his mother." Flick-flick went the cinder-black eyes of the girl, from child to Dane. Again Dane wondered if the girl was teasing her. "You said insights. Like what, for instance? Can you remember any?"

"Once," Dane began, "he was sitting on my lap in the living room. Our living room overlooks a lovely square, with trees. It was summer and they were all green and heavy." She was beginning to get a terrible headache. "Suddenly he said softly, looking out at the trees in a sort of trance, 'I wonder why they don't call the leaves *flowers*. They are a sort of flower, you know.'"

"God!" cried Polly, hugging herself with a delighted little shudder. "He's probably a reincarnation of some lost genius—or poet. Strange! Why, you know, he's the way I expected John to be. I mean, I feel about him what I expected to feel about John." Then she flushed. "There goes Polly the personality-monger, nit-picking and X-raying all over the place. What do you care about my silly analyses? Your husband's an expert in that sort of thing. It's just that I have to have my diversion. You understand. Let's all go outside and eat and drink. The twins are put away for a nap. I don't suppose he'd like one. We fixed a bed for him, but now that I see him, he doesn't look like the nap type."

"No, he likes to stay awake and . . . watch," Dane said. A steady throbbing had set up a regular rhythm just behind her left temple. She regretted having come. It was not the same as it had been yesterday, alone with Polly at the villa.

After lunch, Karl got his crayons, arranged Penelope in a chair and began to get the lie of the land, a full glass of sangria beside him. Even John let himself be persuaded by Polly, who had assumed a solicitous, motherly role toward him, to partake of the alcoholic drink. Now he sat, slightly flushed from it, jotting tiny notes on a piece of paper he had folded many times over to fit his shirt pocket.

"John, you know what you promised," Polly said.

"I haven't forgotten," he replied, looking up with a faint smile. During lunch, Polly had made him agree to take a walk with her and listen to her recurring dream. He had said yes at once, with pleasure. Dane was glad Polly had mentioned the dream yesterday with her intention of asking John. Otherwise it would have seemed to her that Polly was simply being a smart hostess and giving John his chance to shine. "Why don't we go now? Would that suit you?" he said to Polly.

"Great! Want to come, Dane?"

"Thanks. I think I'll take Robin for a

walk in those woods. You two go on." Her head still throbbed. Only now the pain was weighed down with a red coating of sangria.

The two pairs went off in their opposite directions just as Karl said in his musical English, "Penelope darling, lean forward *just* a little. Can you crouch? I want to get that circular feeling in the arms. . . ."

" 'Crouch,' " Dane mimicked, going down through the thicket of pines, toward the sea. Robin held tightly to her hand. "You know what he'll be asking her to do next, don't you?" She looked down at his level gaze. "Sure you do. You know everything. You're just not telling." She was relieved to be away from the others, from the complex little social dramas. "Why do we need to speak of it?" she said. "Just register it, register it in those ice-blue eyes. Kill the Count, kill them all with that blank, relentless gaze." But she felt comradely toward her small stepson. She'd been liking him better ever since he shrieked her back from that solemn swim with John.

At the bottom of the slope, she sat down and leaned her shoulders against the trunk of a pine tree. Fresh air, at last. There was a nice view of the fort from here, and the green sea all around. Robin stood beside her, like a small guard.

"You know something?" she said, exchanging a long look with him. "I prefer your company to all the rest of them up there. You're clean and pure and . . . whatever you are. They're all tainted, or crippled. There's something of decay about all of them. Maybe you know this. Maybe you've seen where all the yak-yakking gets us: nowhere, except around in circles. The yak-yakking's all a cover-up for what's underneath. And *that* keeps flowing along, regardless of us or anything we say about it. Doesn't it?"

To her amazement, he nodded his head very vigorously.

"God! Child, you give me the creeps." She slapped him playfully against the legs.

A little twitch nudged the corners of his mouth. He stepped back, drew in his breath and hit her enthusiastically on the arm. Then he waited, to see what she would do.

She stared, not quite knowing what to make of this new behavior.

He hit her again, harder. And withdrew. And waited.

Experimentally, she hit him on the legs again.

A grin of pure delight spread across his little man's features. Then *Whap!* went the flat of his small hand against her arm.

"Owww!" She pretended great pain.

He danced up and down, making a little chuckle in his throat. He smiled and showed the two rows of even, milk-white teeth. They were so new and perfect, they made the gorge rise in her. She could understand how cannibals could slaver for such a small, perfect morsel. She hit him again, harder, a strange excitement filling her.

"Zose nice plomp leetle legs!" She imitated

the accents of Ramírez-Suárez and the Count Bartolomé. "Do you know what I am going to do to zem?" She raised her hand menacingly.

He giggled and made a small retreat. Waited.

"I am going to *beat* zem!"

He gurgled and danced wildly up and down.

"Yes, you know! I am going to beat zem!" And she reared back as if to deliver a crushing blow—which ended in a tap. She did it again and again. He loved it, the little ritual. It seemed he would never tire of it. What if I should really hit him? she thought. Just knock him flat on his face, with all my strength. A look of incredulity would replace the little smile, the face would redden, there would be the opening chord of the siren scream. She stopped playing with him and grabbed him to her. Put her face in his hair.

He whacked her again, really hard, on the arm. It really hurt. Tears sprang to her eyes. "Damn you, that hurt, friend." She held him at arm's length and looked into the smiling face. "Did you want to hurt me?"

He regarded her with the blue eyes and let the smile fade back into those regions from which it so seldom came. She was sorry that their good moment was past. Her head hurt. Which of them had broken the mood? She couldn't remember.

"Ah, hell," she murmured, pulling him down on her knees. He let himself be arranged, the back of his head to her. The two of them sat looking out at the sea. John was good with people's dreams. Every morning at home, she told him hers. She liked mornings best. John needed very little sleep and rose early, before daylight usually. When he left the bed, the mattress winged upward, she felt afloat in a warm private vessel, which she would ride back into heavily populated dreams. He'd wake her, running upstairs before the arrival of his last morning patient—on the mornings he had one—and sit on the edge of the bed, dressed and in authority. "Where would you like to go to lunch?" he'd say; they usually went out to lunch. And she would lie there, musing in the bedclothes, feeling like an indulged child. "How about that new place that just opened on the King's Road?" or, "I am sick of meat, aren't you? Let's go to that little vegetarian place at World's End." "Fair enough," he'd say. "Did you have any dreams?" She *always* dreamed. Always had. She could remember dreams she'd dreamed at three, although she remembered very little of her age-three waking life. She dreamed of violence, flatteries, threats, deficiencies, missed trains, math courses she'd signed up for and forgotten to attend until exam day, or rapes, embarrassments, food. She carried on long conversations with girls she had hated in school and ended up embracing them and complimenting them and becoming their friend. She'd made love to women and begged all sorts of filthy creatures to rape her; she'd kissed beautiful men only to have their teeth fall out in her mouth; she'd grown huge flowers of flesh from her skull, her hair had come out in great patches; she had gone to visit her father who had died and lived in a roof garden in dryest Italy; she had given birth to a strange little animal which she had crushed in her hand. John was fascinated by her dreams. He had become schooled in their hieroglyphics and his comments on them were to her like those illuminating footnotes which prove more interesting than the manuscript itself. "I dreamed of an old Negro man, standing beside a deserted farmhouse in the middle of nowhere. I think he had blue eyes. He was looking off into the distance and I felt love and awe for him. I wanted to fall down and worship him, or cry," she would say. That time, John had suggested she get dressed quickly and take out her pencils and *draw* the old Negro, just as she had remembered him from the dream. The picture had turned out well. She was no artist, but it had contained some of the mystique, transferred hot from the dream. Sometimes she typed up her dreams, if they'd affected her deeply. She and John would read over them together. "Why *dry?*" John had asked about the dream of her father, dead, living in a roof garden where nothing grew. "Don't you see?" he said. She clapped her hand over her mouth. "My God!" she cried then. How could she leave John? Who else could footnote her dreams?

They had long lunches, commenting on the quality of the food. "We shall have to come here again this week," or, "The noodles or whatever they were in that lasagna were sort of Lyons Corner Housey. I feel bloated. Let's just have a salad for supper." And then they would walk slowly home—John's afternoon patients never came before two—stopping to look in antique shops ("I have been looking for years for one of those green-shaded student lamps." John had bought it for her at once. Fifteen pounds. Wrap it up and carry it home. That makes one afternoon bright) and the record shop where John bought a record almost every day (Joan Baez, Poulenc, Vaughan Williams' songs of an English countryside, *more* Bach, or one of his sons, African tribal music—his tastes spread out, chaotic, without bounds, like the rest of him) and finally, the big event of their day: the bookstore. There was one at either end of the King's Road, another in the middle, and here they would enter together, going their separate ways at the threshold—each a competent athlete in his own right. She went first to novels, he to philosophy and psychology; they came together at science fiction. Often he arrived with a book, which he held out to her: "I thought you might enjoy this. Have you ever read it? No? It's your sort of thing." And it would be that, exactly: her sort of thing. Perhaps literature, perhaps not, but always setting the curious vibrations working in her soul. He had shown her (and bought for her) *Childhood's End, Voyage to Arcturus, Wisdom, Madness and Folly, Operators and Things, The Ha-Ha* and *Memoirs of My Nervous Illness,* all accounts of journeys into the future, the imagination or insanity. He had interested her in Hölderlin by translating a single couplet: "Where the greatest danger lies, there is also the salvation": in Blake by telling her how the boy was thrashed by his father for seeing a treeful of angels in Dulwich. John knew every detail of Nietzche's fall from the tightwire of sanity, of Rimbaud's startling abdication from poetry at twenty-one and the terrible business about the leg, which finally killed him.

She pressed her headache into Robin's soft hair. "What shall I do, little sage?" she said. "I am divided against myself." The child with his back to her suddenly tensed as he looked out to sea. She looked, too, and saw a lovely sleek white yacht crossing the line where water marked sky. Where did it go? Algiers, maybe. Or down to the Strait of Gibraltar, where it would turn right for Lisbon or left for the Canaries. What difference did its destination make, so long as it cut so smoothly and arrogantly through the green sea? What shore watcher was to know whether the crew toasted one another from golden goblets, laughing at the waves, or languished below the deck in the throes of some fearful plague.

Together, Dane and Robin followed the progress of the yacht. She stroked the back of his neck. "What a lovely boat, Robin."

He turned and drilled into her with the blue eyes.

"Are you telling me I should be like the boat? Do you think I should?"

For the second time with her, he nodded.

"Maybe you'll be my little Ouija board," she said, hugging him to her. "But what are you going to do about my headache?"

Chapter
Eleven

"I'm sorry I dragged you into that. The whole thing was a bore," she said, as they were walking the long way round the cove back to the hotel. Penelope they'd left behind; Karl's model had accepted the Heykoops' supper invitation.

"No it wasn't," he said. "It was interesting. I liked her. Besides, I think I have worked out my pattern I was telling you about last night. Dane, I am pretty sure I have found the basic pattern of human thought."

"When did you find it?" she asked, rather jealously.

"I'd been getting precipitations all afternoon. Then, when Polly took me off on the walk, it suddenly formed. Presto! Just like that in my head. It's in the shape of a snowflake."

"I don't think I want to see that woman anymore. She's too nosy. She said you were *shy*."

"Well, I am." He laughed. "Hadn't you noticed? I found her quite sympathetic. She likes you, too."

"What's in the form of a snowflake?" She changed the subject back again.

"The pattern of human responses. Roughly the shape of a snowflake: the same symmetry. A sort of complex circle. The circle's the real point, however. The reason I'd been stuck was, I'd been trying to arrange human responses up and down a ladderlike scale."

"I don't understand, about the circle." Every time her sandals slapped the pavement, her head gave an echoing throb. She hadn't asked Polly for aspirin. She hadn't wanted to give her any more fodder for her personality studies.

"There are certain basic responses, common to us all. Yes? Love, hate, so on . . ."

"Yes." She wasn't sure about love.

"All right," he said, warming to his subject. "Now, my point is this: there are only a limited number of these responses. In fact, there are under a hundred. (That's the responses *with* their opposites. Each response has an opposite: joy has grief; praise, blame, and so on.) Do you see?"

"Joy has grief. Yes . . ."

"What I didn't know until this afternoon was this: these responses can be arranged meaningfully on a circular scale. They can be assigned values on a scale progressing from the human around to the spiritual. Imagine a simple circle, at first. Now. At the top of this circle, write 'Human.' At the bottom, 'Spiritual.' On the right of the circle, to the east, write 'Negative.' On the left, to the west, write 'Positive.' All right so far?"

"Yes," she said, although she'd lost him to the east. If she had said no, he would have begun again from the beginning. Robin walked along beside her, clutching her hand. What did he think of all this?

"Good. Now, a fully constructive sequence starts at 'Human' and works down the positive side to 'Spiritual.' And—*this is important—each step becomes available only after one has taken the step before.* The very first step is a sort of human 'Aha!' a bald recognition that something material exists. One needs to take this step, relative to any part of life, before anything further becomes possible. After this, one works through all types of attitude and activity, humanly speaking, then on to the spiritual attitudes toward each item: first aesthetic, then philosophical, then transpersonal. Take love, for example. After you have become capable of understanding and practicing love of another human being, you can go on to compassionate love, love of a person or thing because it *is*, then love of all things in the universe because they are." He was getting excited. She could not look at his face.

Coming toward them from the bottom of the hill was an ancient creature, scarcely human, dressed in black rags. There was something the matter with its legs. "What was Polly's recurring dream?" Dane asked.

"Oh, it was—Look, let me tell you later. This is more important. You are moving along on this evolutionary scale of responses, you see. Doing this properly—which few, if any, have ever done—you will find that each new attitude or response is not substituted for the last, but added onto it."

She stopped to remove a rock from her sandal. The sun disappeared behind a villa.

"As you complete each level, if you're doing it right, your attitude toward it is complete and joyful."

The scarecrow figure was a crippled old woman. Her eyes riveted on Robin, she dragged her crooked legs up the hill toward them.

"Each level is heavily booby-trapped, however. Each single component (or response) is so enormous that you could spend your entire life dealing with just it, working within its sphere of influence, exhausting all its variations, dramatizing it—we've all seen people make life styles out of Shame or Generosity or Power. It's easy to get stuck in one response, rather than becoming bigger than it."

The breeze whipped at his thick black hair, rearranging it in its usual wildness which complimented the craggy features. Gone was his lopsided, wet-combed look, now that there was no one to see.

"Another thing to beware of: the 'Human' and 'Spiritual' components are mirror images of each other. You can easily mistake what you're trying to do. Like the man who looks for philosophical insights in sex, or the woman who seeks her individuality in social roles. Last but not least of the dangers is if you make a mess of any 'Positive' component. When you do this, you confuse it with its corresponding 'Negative' and down you go on the circle's 'Negative' side into worse and worse misery.

If someone is not a friend to be loved, he must be an enemy to be hated. If I have not won at love, then I must have failed. And there you have the essential mechanism of despair."

Worse and worse misery . . . her head!

"I'm rather excited about this."

The crippled hag came abreast of them. Dane prayed she wouldn't stop. Such an ill-omened looking thing. Robin pulled back, fascinated. She stopped and grinned toothlessly, then reached out one brown and knotted hand, which she placed on the child's head in a sort of blessing.

"*Dios t'bendiga*," she croaked, grinning at them.

"*Gracias*," said John.

"What's she saying?" Dane muttered.

"Something about God."

John and Dane stood, rather awkwardly, while the old hag took her time about the blessing.

"*El Padre cuidará sus pequeños!*" she cried at last, shaking a finger at them and resuming her painful ascent. Robin kept pulling back to watch her out of sight.

"That's rickets," John said.

They passed Pedro's and came to the crossroads. To the right was the road which led to Count Bartolomé's stables. To the left was the pine-shaded road leading to their hotel. A dusty, doorless bus pulled up at the crossroads with a shrill grinding of gears and disgorged passengers who turned out to be the beautiful French family. They had been on a picnic. The man carried a wicker basket filled with stoppered wine bottles and the remainder of a loaf of bread. His black hair fell forward over his eyes, giving him a rakish, boyish air. The woman carried stacks of clay-colored pottery in her arms and the two children wore new straw sombreros. They had probably bought these in the neighboring village of Felanitx. The family started down the road to the hotel, just ahead of the Empsons. Back to their hot, cramped little rooms, thought Dane, where they were so happy.

"Everything I do or have done is located somewhere in that snowflake," John said. "For instance, I know now that all my basic problems have stemmed from efforts to achieve one and the same component, one of the positive spiritual ones."

"Which one?" asked Dane. The Indian-brown muscles of the Frenchman's arm were taut under the weight of the basket. The woman walked with her stomach thrust forward to support the stacks of earthenware. They would return soon to their own bright and sunny French kitchen. She would set the earthenware plates and bowls upon a gay little tablecloth and they would all remember their holiday in Majorca. A tiny wave of nausea welled up in Dane.

"I'd rather not say," John answered. "Not just yet. These words have a real kick to them. They are the basics and so naturally are charged with great emotional content. They're the things we have been trying to achieve, or failing at, all our lives. My word might have the wrong repercussions in you. You might be struggling with it at another level and feel repulsed or degraded by hearing it."

Dane turned to go ahead of him into the circular drive of the hotel. "Oh, for God's sake. If these words are so fucking universal, I hear them in common speech every day."

"Wait," he said, "don't go in yet. Let's walk down to the end of this road. It's the end of the island down there; Mrs. Hart told me there's a nice little harbor with fishing boats."

"My head is about to split open. I feel, any minute, as though a huge black flower were going to burst through my skull and blossom at the expense of my very sanity."

"When did you get your headache?" (He always asked this. It was his theory that if you could trace it back to the moment when it started, and then reconfront that moment, the headache would disappear.)

"When we got to Polly's. I don't remember." The French family continued up the dusty road toward their bare annex.

"Go upstairs and get your Bufferin," he ordered. "Leave him with me. We'll walk down to the little harbor and I'll find your headache for you and drop it into the sea." He rumpled her hair, standing there in the entrance to the drive. "I shan't give up on you," he said. "You're too important to me."

"How? How can I be?" she asked. "I'm a terrible wife. Any other man would be totally alienated from me by now."

"Yes, in some ways you have been terrible," he said. "But some of your terribleness has been extremely generative for me. I've never felt more positive in my life. Look, run fetch your Bufferin, take two, and come back." He held her with his dark eyes. "I'll tell you my word, if you do," he bribed, smiling mischievously.

"Aren't you afraid I'll go up in smoke before your eyes?" she taunted. "Okay. Here, Robin, stay with Daddy."

She hurried into the cool hotel, rather gratified that Robin whined after her. "Stop that, Robin," she heard John say with annoyance. Both of them watched her anxiously into the hotel and would wait just as anxiously for her return.

She took three Bufferins, washed her face and sat down on John's bed, just so they'd have to wait a bit. *The Book of Marriage* lay just beneath the bed, a place marked with a scrap of paper. John had been reading "The Proper Choice of Partners," Count Keyserling's own essay. She found new underlines in black ink: "Generally speaking, only the mother type is suitable for marriage. For it has roots in the primordial nature of man; it typifies responsibility and is therefore serious in character. In the comrade type, man seeks adventure, stimulation and sport . . . the comrade should never become the wife." Underlined with fervor.

Did that mean he agreed with old Keyserling? John often called her his companion and sometimes his baby. She was about as motherly as a stone and about as concerned about it as one. The image of Mrs. Hart suckling two babies at once came back to her, and with it another wave of nausea.

Going down again, she thought: I don't want to walk anywhere to see any nice little harbor. I don't care what his word is. It's something cloying. Don't I know him well enough to know any word which would give him joy would make me sick? When am I going to face it?

Ramírez-Suárez practically pounced on her in the lobby.

"Are you having a nice afternoon, señora?"

She said yes, thank you.

There they were, waiting for her, both of them frowning toward the entrance, waiting for Mother of Stone. They would go for a walk. Paltry. Mrs. Hart came chattering up the drive, accompanied by Mr. von Schirmbeck in white shorts and shirt, swinging along on his crutches. Both their faces were pink, hers from enthusiasm, his from sun.

Dane slipped on the first step outside. She flew through the air and landed on the bottom step on the base of her spine. "*Dear* Mrs. Empson," she heard Mrs. Hart cry. Ramírez-Suárez fluttered down on her like some skinny black bird. I'm going to faint, she thought, starting to swirl. I won't have to go and see the nice boats, after all.

When she opened her eyes again, she was lying at the foot of the steps. The one-legged German was kneeling over her. His eyes were pale, like washed-out granite. "*Geht es Ihnen besser?*" he asked gently.

"I've always liked you, Mr. von Schirmbeck," she said. She was covered in cold sweat.

"That's right, Mrs. Empson," cried Mrs. Hart. She dabbed some fresh-smelling cologne with a handkerchief on Dane's cheeks and forehead. "We all like Mr. von Schirmbeck. Doctor, do we dare move her?"

"I don't see why not. She's had a painful fall, but it will be all right. Dane, are you able to walk to the room?" He bent over her, a dark-eyed, stern man. She felt much closer to Mrs. Hart and Mr. von Schirmbeck.

Everyone helped her to her feet. John and Mrs. Hart went up the stairs with her. The German stayed below, watching them go. Ramírez-Suárez tried to get Robin to accept his help in navigating the stairs in this time of crisis. The child went alone, using his hands on the stair ahead when necessary.

"Do you think the *baby* will be all right?" Mrs. Hart whispered to John. "The second month, isn't it?"

"I should think it would be," John said. "If she lies still for a time, just to make sure."

"Yes, Mrs. Empson, we'll have you straight to bed. You mustn't move until the doctor says you can." The old lady was adamant. It might have been her own baby. For a minute, Dane actually believed in her phantom fetus. Such was the power of Mrs. Hart's concern.

When they were alone, John said, "What happened down there?"

"What do you mean, what happened? Didn't you see?"

"I saw you fall. Why did you fall?"

Why! I slipped, that's why. But he seemed to expect something more dark and complex. Very well. "I suddenly blacked out," she said. "I simply lost consciousness."

"You fainted, or started to faint, *before* you fell?"

"Fainted, or . . . something. I just went away." He was watching her avidly. "It was rather awful, having to come back," she said. She rememberd the gentle concern in the eyes of Mr. von Schirmbeck contrasted to the less friendly scrutiny of her own husband, and began to weep softly.

"Wait. Try and think. How did you 'just go away'?"

"I didn't want to be here anymore. I didn't want to go on. Something inside me abdicated. Will you hand me that little bottle of cologne Mrs. Hart left me?"

Abstracted, he fetched the bottle from the dresser, uncapped it and was about to pour some on his handkerchief for her. "No"—he put the handkerchief away again—"it's too dirty. I'll find something else."

Robin, who had been hovering beside her bed, staring at Dane, suddenly picked up one of his own little socks which lay just beside the closet. He handed it to his father.

"What's this for?" John said.

"It's to rub my face with, silly," Dane said. "Here. Give it to me. Give the sock and the cologne to me." She drenched the little sock and caressed her face with it while Robin watched. "He's the wise one in this family," she said.

John went dark.

"Are you jealous of a little child?" she asked. Then a perfect calm descended upon her. She smiled, unbelieving, and pressed her fingers experimentally to her temples.

"What's the matter?" he said.

"My headache is gone," she said. "Isn't that wonderful?"

Chapter
Twelve

Union. Just as well, perhaps, that she "fell," thus preventing the disclosure of the simple word above. She would read it as another word: *invasion.* Whereas all my efforts have been toward the positive spiritual value, hers have been in opposition to its negative counterpart. It looks as if we shall be chasing round the circle forever, with no meeting place. . . .

So that was his precious word. She might have guessed. The zygote urge again. She lay in the morning sun, in the corner of their balcony. John had taken Robin shopping in the village and she was leafing through his hot-from-the-presses notes. It would have been cooler, much pleasanter, down on the beach, but Mrs. Hart was there, sitting upright on her old army blanket, reading a thin airmail edition of the *Times* which kept trying to flutter away in the breeze. The old lady would be scandalized if she came down to the beach. Women who fell down a flight of stairs in their second month and didn't miscarry at once—like Scarlett O'Hara Butler had done—were supposed to lie still as a corpse and hope against hope that their precious burden had remained undamaged. So, trapped by her own fabrication, Dane broiled unseen on the balcony. (What did he mean: "fell"?)

He must have sat up all night. There were *pages*. At one point he'd drawn a lopsided circle and labeled the parts, then made little weblike lines, like the outermost extensions of a snowflake. On these fine lines were jammed together all sorts of words: "Unworthiness," "affirmation," "abhorrence," "ingratiation," "callousness," "grandiosity," "universal horror" and so on. She could not read them all. Had he discovered something really significant? Would his picture be on the cover of *Time* one day? ("Dr. Empson, Cartographer of Psyches, and his stylish wife, Dane, surrounded at Kennedy Airport by . . .") Or was he just another Julian Glover, the crackpot in plus fours and gaiters who used to come and bother them at the magazine with his latest "inventions" which he urged them to write up: a man's bicycle with detachable crossbar so ladies could ride; ladies' hair curlers, each with its separate alarm bell, since some hair got dry on the head before other hair; milk bottles with ounce, cup and pint measurements marked on them . . . ad infinitum. Nothing wrong with these things, but who needed them? They were esoteric, superfluous to the lives most people lived. ("Oh God, Dane, Julian Glover just came in. It's your turn to talk to him.") Could John's snowflake be useful? Would it make anyone happier or more effective?

Farther on, he laspsed into the personal:

I wanted to say it all to D first, as a bridge to saying it to the world. Now, I suppose, lacking the bridge . . .

Had he given up on her, then?

. . . I shall look for one within myself . . . [illegible] mother to my visions, I shall give birth to them myself. Visions, like children, must be nurtured, encouraged, tolerated in their imperfect embryonic stages. D will not permit the child in anything. She wants finished products only.

Day after tomorrow, after breakfast, they would all climb into a taxi and drive to Palma airport. Penelope would chirp bright comments on the passing scenery of her mind, perhaps punctuated with nostalgic little sighs for her holiday lover. John in his dark suit would face front, smiling abstractly, a large dark cat sitting on his snowflake. They would board their charter plane and fly away from the sun, across the jewel-green Mediterranean, the white-tipped strip of Pyrenees, across the antique-yellow landscape of Spain, up the coast of neat French farmlands, then crossing the wintry-blue channel into the land of clouds from which they came. The engines would subdue themselves to wet whispers as the aircraft descended, all but grazing the rows of dull red rooftops of brown Surrey houses. The passengers would stir resolutely, their suntans hovering already a few centimeters from their faces, and gather up their holiday accumulations, so superfluous-seeming in this sober light. She would finger her seat belt, searching her imagination for something to look forward to, something to guide her life by. She would turn and look down into the eyes of the child: blue mirrors, reflecting her own question. Penelope was much easier to imagine getting reestablished after the holiday. Dane could "do" Penelope far better than she could do herself. Simple: They'd drop Penelope off at her tiny flat, where she'd run upstairs, have a moment of depression when she faced the emptiness, the soot which had gathered on the sill. Then she'd rally—her dresses must be taken out and hung in the closet without any doors. After everything was unpacked, she'd possibly fling herself down on her frilly bedspread and weep for the passage of time, for the ephemerality —like Dutch tulips—of Dutch lovers, for the termination of all holidays. Then her stomach would rumble and she'd get up, wash her face (admiring her tan in the bathroom mirror) and go and heat a tin of beans. She would appear in Hatchard's bright and early, her Majorcan holiday the big topic of conversation among her fellow clerks. And when she began feeling the phenomenon of her existence too rawly, or when her horoscope in the *Evening Standard* had been particularly ominous, why then she could simply ring up John and ask for another appointment at one-third of the regular price. Soon she would have a new boyfriend, and she would ask John, "Do you think I ought to sleep with him?" and John would say, "What do *you* think?" Next would come the questions: "Do you think I should marry him; he's awfully sweet?" "Do you think I'll be a good mother?" "Do you think I'm too lenient with the child?" "Really? You do think it will be all right if I have another?" "Do you think they'll get into Oxford?" "Maybe I'm silly, but you know, I sometimes feel this *tiny* jealousy toward my sons' wives. Is that natural? Oh, good." "Tell me truthfully, John: do you think I spoil my grandchildren?"

Etc., etc., etc. Penelope was a competent swimmer—not Olympic material, not the kind to put on a diver's mask and shoot below the surface to seek the caves of lost Atlantis. She'd keep on doing her hundred and forty strokes, every so often looking down and seeing the great mysterious expanse of water churning round her. "Oh my God! I'm swimming! That's water! Will I be able to go on swimming, do you think?" she'd exclaim, and John or somebody would come by at just that moment in a boat and call, "Of course you can, dear. Look! You're over halfway there." And on she'd go, with her complacent long-wearing breast stroke, oblivious to all the dangers and ecstasies beneath her, the strange shapes, the ancestors and the enemies of man. And she would make it over the drowned corpses of many others.

What would John do on Sunday when he got back to the house in Chelsea? Easy. Put on Beethoven. Fetch his clipboard, rip open a fresh ream of unlined foolscap and sit down on the garish green sofa with a sigh and the opening of grand chords and begin to write.

Getting back to herself: she would have to start somewhere on the return. And the return was a *given*, wasn't it? Return to what? Well, she knew herself well enough to know her first urge would be to unpack, to put everything back where it was, to reinstate herself in her space again. First to unpack, then to go around from window to window, dusting two weeks of London's black soot from the sills, from the surfaces of the brown furniture. Oh, and there was Robin's bed to contend with. He'd wet it the night before they left. They were late getting started and she'd only had time to pull the sheets off and tip back the mattress. It was as if she smelled it in the air, here on the balcony: the sour smell coming from the mattress, the smoky dampness that hung about the rooms in spite of their new paint, in spite of her hundred little decorations and renovations. John had actually wept when she took down the Montmartre poster, yellowed at the edges, and put up a neat framed print of her own. He and Vanessa had loved each other, that spring in Montmartre. "Are you saying that you still love her?" "No, but it's all that's left of what we had." "But the poster's old, John. It's a mess. It attracts dust. Can't you see that?" "Yes, I can see it. I suppose I wished you'd shown some sort of tenderness as you took it down. . . ."

After she tidied up the place, she would take a bath. What would Robin be doing, all this time? She'd forgotten him. Running up and down the dark hallways? Sitting in a corner, stuffing himself with Smarties? Looking at colored pictures of advanced cancer in his father's old medical books? She was unable to place him. And yet the answer to her future seemed to be contained in those big staring eyes. She returned again and again to them whenever her imagination balked. Their blue depths seemed to know, assess, pity, deplore— yet also, sometimes, absolve. She felt absolved when he offered that little sock. He had summed it up in an instant: what she needed. When he handed that sock to John, he was the comforter in that room. He was the parent. Perhaps she and Robin would beome mutes together. Walking up and down the King's Road, mother and son, making everyone un-easy with the two pairs of silent, watching orbs. The power of silence was not to be underrated. One time she had seen an Ingmar Bergman film about a woman who wouldn't talk. She drove everyone around her mad—including the nurse.

There was a pert knock at the door of their room. Dane expected the maids, so didn't go to answer.

But Polly Heykoop came out, wearing a black sundress and a wide-brimmed black straw hat. She looked the freckled young witch, on her way to a sabbat. Under her arm she carried a photograph album. "Well, I've tracked you to your lair," she cried in her hoarse satiric voice. "I was on my way here and I saw John in the village. He said you'd fallen downstairs and busted your ass."

"John would never say 'ass.' Hey, take off that hat; you look exactly like a witch." Dane tried to get her bearings under cover of random chitchat. Having decided never to see Polly again, it hadn't occurred to her that Polly would come to see her. "I'm just lying around," she said. "I don't want to go down to the beach, because there's this dear old lady who's taken a shine to me. She saw me fall and expects me to stay in bed all day."

"What a nice balcony!" said the other, looking around. Those cinder-bright eyes didn't miss much. "Can I sit under the umbrella?"

"Sure. It's John's study. He writes under it. I've just been reading a rough draft of his latest idea. He wanted to see what I'd think of it. Excuse me, I'll be back." She went into the room and put John's notes where she'd found them, under his clothes in the suitcase. Before she went back out, she stood in front of the mirror and practiced a Robin look. Ice-blue eyes. Brrr. She wouldn't stay long if somebody looked at her like that.

"What's in your album?" she asked Polly, who had put it on the table and folded her nail-bitten fingers primly on top of it. "You look like you've stolen state secrets or something."

"Pull up a chair. It's what I came to show you." The dark girl glowed with mischief.

"I can't resist state secrets," Dane said. She sat down next to Polly. The two of them bent quaintly forward over the black-and-gold album.

"I know you can't. Ready?" Polly turned to the first page, which was black, except for a white-inked inscription: "For Karl."

"Oh, how touching," said Dane. They both laughed. "Has he seen it?"

"Not yet. It's his sixtieth-birthday pressent." There was a demon in Polly's grin. She turned the page. There was an eight-by-ten photograph, rather grainy, of a man embracing a woman. "Terrible shot. I get better as I go along. I'm a self-taught photographer. The pictures are in chronological order. This was my first attempt." Beneath the picture was "Michelle," printed in the white ink, and a date three years before.

"Just a stupid model," said Polly. "Not very significant. But a transgression, nevertheless. So, old Michelle, we shall preserve you and your ephemeral beauty."

Gaily she flipped the page. The man in this photo was unmistakably Karl. He wore a neat little beard and sat in a deck chair on a terrace—the terrace at the villa. His back was to the camera but his profile (laughing) was turned to a lovely dark-haired girl who was sitting at his feet. One of her hands had disappeared beyond his visible leg. She was obviously fondling his crotch. "I almost fell out of the upstairs window getting this. It was my first experience with a telephoto lens (Karl thinks it's so healthy for me to have a hobby, he forks out for anything I want to help me get beautiful shots of canals and boats and little darlings playing in the park.) I was supposed to be upstairs taking a nap; I was very pregnant with the twins that summer." "Nancy," said the white ink, and inclusive summer dates, three years before.

The next page featured a voluptuous raven-haired beauty, naked from the waist up. She was shrugging into a blouse and taking her time about it. "That was a big year for brunettes," said Polly. "Birgit—November," said the white ink. Three years old. "I got there too late for the main performance—they were at Karl's studio—because I had to get a neighbor to come and sit with the babies. It was raining and I got these—there were more, but she looks best in this one—from a fire escape. Don't you think she looks alive, in that shot? Those pouty lips with just a highlight of wet on the lower one. Full bloom of youth, sex, all that."

"She *is* nice," agreed Dane, intrigued by Polly's matter-of-factness. The visit had taken an interesting turn.

"Very nice! And won't she be nice in thirty years! Those pouty cheeks and pointy breasts will be down to her ankles when Karl and I flip through these pages together for the first time. Eh, Birgit?" Polly stuck out her tongue at the picture with happy malice.

"I think I understand you," Dane said.

"Do you see it?" The two women looked at each other.

"God, you *are* a witch," Dane said, smiling collusively.

"Of course I'm a witch. A witch who wants to survive. Do you think he'll like his little gift?"

"I don't know. I don't think he'll be angry. I think he'll be . . . flattered."

"He'll be flattered! He'll love it!" cried Polly.

"He will! Husband, I have sailed along in the wake of your transgressions and saved for you these sea shambles of discarded mer-maids," Dane chanted. The two of them giggled insanely. "Go on, turn the page, I'm dying to see the next exposure." They were off again.

"Sonja, Karen, Louisa . . ." Polly read.

"How many are there?" said Dane. "Ooooh, there's a shocking one. Did you hang by your heels to get that one?"

At last there were no more. The last page had "Penelope" inked neatly at the bottom, with two inclusive dates: last night's and to-morrow's.

"Is this *our* Penelope?" Dane said.

"Sure as hell is. I can't do any developing til we get back to Amsterdam. All my stuff's there. I'm a little worried about last night's roll. Last night's *roll!* God, I'm funny today! I'm not sure there was enough light. The fools were outside in the pine needles. She wouldn't keep still, either: kept rolling over and over him, with her hair flying in her eyes, looking desperate. I was 'putting the twins to bed.' He gets more careless as the years go on. But that's all right: my pictures get better. To-night I have a plan: if I can maneuver them inside the villa and get outside, then I ought to have something printable. He likes a bit of light, anyway. Still"—she bit her lip—"there will be techinical problems."

"You actually *want* them to make a good picture for you," said Dane.

"Naturally. Oh, I see what you mean. I did start the album in a kind of spite, but now it's become a thing in its own right. I want to make it nice and thick, with clear, sharp-focused shots. I want to catch these women with their souls exposed. I want to turn the pages for old Karl and say, 'Look, honey, how she wanted you.' It's to be my memorial to his virility."

"And you are wrapped up in it, just as he is wrapped up in his art," said Dane.

"Yes. It's very absorbing. When I'm trying to get a good shot, I forget I'm watching my husband make love with another woman."

"The two things are separated," said Dane.

"Yes, I see it."

"You read me very well," said Polly. "I want the chance to show how well I can read you." Her face was really quite pale beneath the black straw brim. It was the heavy layer of freckles which gave the illusion of a tan.

"What do you mean? What kind of chance?" Dane withdrew a little; she leaned back in her chair away from Polly. "It's not too cool out here, is it?"

"You watched me beat my children and clapped from the road," said Polly softly. "You listened to the story of how I met my husband at the fort. You looked at my album, my secret project. I have been a good performer and you have been a most attentive spectator. If we're going to get on with the friendship, it's my turn to be the spectator."

"Wait a minute." Dane stopped the glittering probe of those black eyes with a Robin look. "Are you saying you want some sort of intimate exchange? Do you think *I* have some kind of album? Look, I understand. You've bared your secret to me and you're bound to feel exposed. You want to make it even."

"I don't feel exposed. I figured I'd have to go first. I know you put on the big stoic act, so I was willing. But you can level with me. We could make it easier for each other. I figured it all out, lying in bed last night."

"How can I level with you more than I have done? My life's not full of intrigue, like yours. It's really quite ordinary."

"I'm sorry. I don't believe you. What about—oh, *why* do you make me go all the way? What about Robin, for instance?"

"What about him?" Dane said. She was uncomfortable now, but she looked at the other woman unflinchingly.

"Well, Penelope spilled the beans last night at supper. She was so nervous and uncertain, wedged between lover and wife. She talked too much. She said you'd only been married ten months—I wasn't even probing; I'd decided not to, because I had plans for our friendship. Anyway, I said, winking at Karl, 'Ha, ha, we were almost like them. Only we beat our kids to the altar by six weeks.' But then she went all puzzled and started to explain, caught herself up and stopped. Then, later, she said something about you only having been in England a year before you met John. So then I said, 'Wait, I'm all confused, Penelope; you'll be doing us all a favor if you straighten this thing out,' and Karl pinched her under the table and said, 'Yes, beauty, do tell my wife. She is not happy until she has the lives of everyone pieced together,' and that, of course, did the trick. Penelope blushed charmingly, demurred until another pinch, then came out with it. When she finished, I clapped my hand to my mouth and said, 'Oh, of course, I believe Dane *did* imply all this to me, only I wasn't listening carefully. Penelope was therefore relieved from the onerous burden of gossiping about her friends."

"That was considerate of you," Dane said. "You're the perfect hostess." Where, where, *where* was John?

"No, I had a motive. I want her to come back to the villa, in case the other shots didn't turn out. I knew she wouldn't if she felt guilty."

"And you're honest, too," said Dane. "I can see you have all the credentials for a good friend. Robin's mother was a doctor. She and John worked together and had a brief love affair. John didn't want to marry her because she wasn't his equal. So after she had the child, she put him in a foster home to spite John and left the country. If he wanted Robin, he'd have to go through years of red tape to get him. Visits from social workers, the whole bit. It's going to be a terrible struggle. More people than yourself will be poking around our lives. If I don't go around showing the dirty linen, it's for Robin's sake. One mother wouldn't claim him, I'll be damned if I'll make it two. What's so important about biological motherhood, anyway? There. That's my revelation: my stepson on a platter. Enjoy, enjoy."

"I don't see why you have to be so angry," Polly said. "I'm not a—some kind of monstrous scavenger. I just thought I'd take the aggressive, try to knock down some of those silly barriers people set up at the beginning." Then, incredibly, she added, "Besides—I've got to say it—I don't think the thing about Robin is your photograph album. And yes, I *do* think you have one, and I'd love to see it."

"I don't have to take this," Dane said. She got up and went into the room.

Polly followed her. Dane picked up a science fiction, lay down on the bed and pretended to read.

The shy, hoarse voice said sorrowfully, "What I'm after is a friend. I don't have a single woman friend—"

"Well, it's no wonder," said Dane, "with your peculiar way of going about getting one." She put the book down. The girl no longer threatened her.

"I guess I want to go straight to the heart of things," said Polly, wrapping one sandaled foot around her other leg. She looked about ten, like an orphan child of ten.

"Like a tiger goes straight for the throat."

"It's just that there is so little time," said Polly. "And I sensed this forthrightness about you, at the first, when you were standing there in the road. I thought: With such a friend I could complete myself."

"Can't you complete yourself with your husband?" Dane said, a bit of the tiger herself. "John is my friend," she added, rather triumphantly. "He's all the friend I need."

"I don't think you can do it with a husband. If you do, the other suffers. There are certain places where husbands and wives

215

shouldn't travel together—certain areas—or the whole thing goes blah."

"Where?" said Dane. "What places?"

"In—in that area of *analysis* about relationships. At least, the relationship you have with each other. As soon as you start analyzing it, you—each of you—lose some of your otherness, that part of the male or that part of the female that the other keeps straining for. The unknowable part. I don't want to know all of Karl. When he comes to me, I sometimes feel he's a wonder alien, someone I'll never interpret, another species altogether. It's only when we make love that we're really together. And we're something else then. We're something other than either of us. I would never sit around with Karl and say, 'What is this otherness, dear, that makes you so attractive? Let's analyze it —A, B, C—and give it a name.' But the analyzing has to come because I'm a Western woman and because I never know what I think or believe until I've thought it aloud to someone else. That somebody shouldn't be my husband but *should* be my equal. Maybe even *more* than me. Has got to understand and contribute and, perhaps, even go beyond. I think *you* could go beyond the usual limits."

"I think your ideas are beautifully antique, Polly. But I can't agree about this otherness thing. If you are limitless—and all complex people are—then you'll never touch bottom, you'll never give yourself away and lose all your mystery—or otherness, as you put it." This was John's argument, not her own! But with it, she'd got the other off her back; old

Polly had lost the scent, wandering past John's words in search of a friend. "Why did you think I could go beyond the usual limits; what do you mean by that?"

"The first day. You said risky things. You clapped. You bypassed the usual conventional stuff. You seemed to say truths out loud, as they came to you, whether or not they were pleasant truths."

"Like what?"

"Oh—I can't remember. At one point you said you were taking the afternoon off from your child and you implied that children were not all comfort and joy. Maybe I was just reading things into you. Shit, maybe I was just lonely."

"I would be the first to say children are not comforts and joys. I don't know about the rest. Maybe you *were* reading, just a little."

"It was that you were capable of saying much more. Like, you could have said, 'He's not really my child, and because he's not there are these strange problems.' And then we could have discussed them. And then I could have told you what kind of problems there are when they are your own. We would have filled in each other's blanks and each been enriched by the other's experience. We would forget pride and 'good manners' and all that stiff-upperlip crap and simply go digging for truth, help each other survive. With a husband you have to keep up appearances, I don't care who says not. They have their aura, we have ours. They are eternally different auras. Why won't you admit you have problems? Everything's not right with you. Yesterday you looked like a hunted woman. There are things between you and John—Look, I observed him on that walk. I think he's kind and I think he's smart as hell, but there are bound to be problems, living with someone like him—"

"Stop, please. I refuse to discuss my marriage with anyone except John. We are friends, comrades. We do sit around and analyze. We have our own thing; you and Karl have yours—"

"But does it work? Can you really feel the *other*, as well?" Ferret, ferret went the cinder-bright eyes, little squirrels nibbling for nuts.

They would not find anything. Winter had already come. It lay like silver-blue ice in Dane's eyes. Wise Robin, inspire me: show me how to freeze this room.

"It works—sublimely," Dane said, rather breathlessly. "It is sacred to me."

"Then," replied the other, after a pause, "I guess I'm the one who ought to go and shoot myself. My husband's not enough, I still need a friend." She was on the verge of tears. The witch was going to weep.

"Oh, relax," said Dane, more friendly. "Let's all go out and get drunk tonight. Let's be friends for the rest of the holdiay. Come to visit us in London and I'll take you to the Wax Museum. We can talk about art and music—and even old Penelope, how she's faring in her post-album days. I'm just a cold stone, Polly. My father is a military man and raised me like crew. John is my only confidant, but I could have fun with you."

"I'm very funny," said Polly, trying to

smile under her witch hat. "That's my recurring dream, you know. The one I told John. In the dream, I'm to meet Karl at the Rijks Museum—that's the place with all the Rembrandts. But the guard won't let me in unless I do a jig and keep on dancing the whole time inside. So I'm bouncing from room to room, laughing and singing, searching for Karl, who's in there *somewhere*, and I know the guards are behind me, with knives, ready to kill me on the spot the minute I stop dancing."

"God. How interesting. What did John say?"

"He said, 'Do you think being an entertaining person is an act of generosity or of self-abasement?' Then he snapped his fingers and said, 'Of course, yes!' and went off into his own little world."

"So he didn't help?"

"Oh, yes. The entertainer thing. That's my bit. I see now. Only, isn't the court jester the loneliest person at court?"

"Depends on the king, I should think," answered Dane. Winning was too easy now. "Let's meet for drinks, even old Penelope, after dinner," she said graciously. The room was hot. She wanted to go down before lunch, hobbling tentatively for Mrs. Hart, of course, and sit like a pale, cool invalid, drinking a gin and lime.

"I was coming to ask *you* that," said Polly. "But I had ulterior motives—you see, I just can't stop baring myself, even if you are an old stone. There's a little dance band coming up from Palma, because it's Friday. I was thinking of a sort of collaboration, actually. At the end of the evening, I would ask you all back to the villa. Only you would beg off, saying your back hurt from the fall, or something. Then I could urge Penelope to come back with us. *She* won't be tired. Not with him around. Then I'll leave the two of them alone because *I* get tired, see, and slip upstairs and get my camera and invent a way to get them from outside. I wonder if you feel that would be collaborating with me too much."

"I can do that, Polly. I can gang up with you against the whole world, only—no state secrets." It was a little like being a monarch, granting small favors which would in no way diminish oneself. "I'll be glad to help you get your album. I have faith in it. It will outlast us all. I'm only sorry I disappointed your expectations. You saw the outline of a fine person, but one who isn't me."

"Oh, I think it *was* you," said the other. Like two quick flies, the black eyes came to rest on Dane, crawled hungrily, fondly, over a morsel under glass, gave up at last. "Seven-thirty? Eight? At Pedro's." With a little smile and a shrug, she let herself out of the room.

"Robin has brought you a present," said John. "Want to give Mommy the little statue?"

Importantly, the child handed over a small wooden icon of a holy man. He was about a foot high, carved of dark pine, with blank eyes and an inscrutable little smile.

"Oh, thank you, Robin! I love him." She hugged the child to her; rigid, he allowed him-

220

self to be fondled. "But who is he? He's adorable. Such a strange little face. Brrr. It looks so wise. He looks like he knows all the secrets. Speaking of secrets, Penelope told ours to the Heykoops."

"What secret?"

"That Robin wasn't mine. Polly came by to pass on the news that she *knew*."

"That sort of thing is bound to come up," he said. "You shouldn't let it affect you. How did you feel when she told you she knew?"

"I felt exposed. After all, I've been trying to act like a mother to him."

"You put too much emphasis on—"

"Biological motherhood. That's what I told Polly. But I don't believe it. The problems are different when the child is not your own." Now she quoted Polly!

"Either way, there are problems. There are always problems. I should think you'd find your sort more interesting. They're not the run-of-the-mill problems of every mother. They're between you and Robin as individuals."

"All the same, it would be simpler if he were my own. It would be more organic. There would be all those centuries of racial memory to fall back on when I lost my way."

"No child would be 'your own,'" he said. "It would be itself."

"Then can you say that Robin is no more to you than someone else's child would be?"

"It wouldn't matter, no, if he were produced by another man's sperm. What he is to me stems from his being Robin. As an individu-

221

al, he happens to have many of the traits I had as a child. I like to think I'll be able to anticipate his needs better than any other man could."

"He wouldn't have *been* like you if he hadn't had your chromosomes."

"Yes, he might have. Many children are totally unlike their parents. I was nothing like my parents. On the other hand, you often see people who are strangely akin, in looks, personality, everything, and aren't even vaguely related."

"You don't believe that. You might believe it intellectually, but you don't feel it."

"All right," he said pleasantly. "Excuse me a moment." He went to the bathroom, leaving her in the lurch, like a tiresome patient who's gone beyond the end of his fifty-five minutes.

She wandered back out on the balcony and leaned over the wall. The Frenchman was sitting on his towel, weaving some bits of straw together for the amusement of the two children. The woman stood some distance away, absently playing with her dark hair as she chatted with a handsome blond woman. This second woman, Dane recognized with a shock, was none other than Penelope. The two of them were talking! Penelope and Dane's Frenchwoman. How could they? The Frenchwoman did not speak English. Did Penelope speak the Frenchwoman's language? Incredible. But there they were, down there together: gab-gab-gab. What were they talking about? It diminished the Frenchwoman for Dane. And 'there was old Penelope, breast-stroking in the warm sea of her life, unconscous of the Frenchwoman who had illumined Dane's dream. To Penelope, it was just another chitchat with a pretty woman with a husband and children from France. That should have been me down there, thought Dane.

"There's a little guidebook that goes with your statue," John said, coming out to her. He handed her an orange-and-yellow booklet entitled "Majorca." "If you'll look on page ten, there's a little something on your man. His name is Ramón Lull, the island's famous thirteenth-century mystic." Dane flipped quickly through the book. "The fellow certainly got around," John went on. "He perfected the compass, taught Arabic, wrote a book on the art of finding truth, went to Africa as a missionary, discovered nitric acid and was stoned to death, a martyr at age eighty-four. . . ."

"In his youth," she read, "Ramón was a wild profligate. Riding his horse through the city of Palma one day, he spied a beautiful young lady entering a church. He spurred his horse and galloped in, through the great west doorway, to where she was kneeling. When he importuned her with his demands, she uncovered her bosom and displayed a breast that was being slowly consumed by a loathsome cancer. He repented and set his love on Jesus Christ Who can never disappoint."

"Oh, how ghastly," she said. "Oh—" Her eyes filled with tears. She turned away.

"What is it?" John said.

"It's so true."

"What is?"

"The disillusionment. It's universal. It's eternal. It's horrible."

"It's only a marked-off place on the negative side of the circle," John said, smiling. "On the other side, to balance it, and finally to embrace it, are bigger, positive concepts. It is impossible to emancipate oneself from being disillusioned."

"How?"

"If you get rid of your illusions, there can be no *dis*-illusion." He said it so simply, like a child reciting from a primer.

"Words, words, words," crooned Dane, holding the little wooden statue. Like Robin, he neither cuddled nor resisted.

Chapter
Thirteen

"That's Betelgeuse," said John. He leaned back in his chair and pointed beyond the colored lanterns strung around Pedro's patio to the reddish star.

"Yes, just look at them all," said Penelope, meaning the stars, but her eyes were actually on Karl, who had spotted his old friend Count Bartolomé at the bar and gone at once to talk to him. Karl did not do much to conceal his dislike for John. There was a deep animosity between them. It seemed to have developed since their meeting yesterday at the villa. John had a way of tacitly excluding Karl from conversations, as thought the Dutchman were a mere friendly animal and could not be expected to understand. Karl got his own back by being sarcastic—even rude. His last words before going to see the Count at the bar had been: "Well, I shall leave you ladies." Now he lounged comfortably against the bar, easy in the company of the riding master and the bartender, who was stroking a little cat in his arms.

"I wish somebody would explain to me about red giants and white dwarfs," said Polly in her hoarse voice.

"The red giants have a lower surface temperature," said John. "Thus, their redness. They have a very high luminosity. That's why we can see them from far away. The white dwarfs are really collapsed stars—"

"Collapsed stars," murmured Polly. "I like the sound of those. They sound elegiac."

"They're pieces of whole stars which were once extremely hot. They have very low luminosities and must be quite close before we can see them with the naked eye."

"Astronomy sounds so interesting. I suddenly want to rush out and take a course in it!" cried Polly. "Yet I know if I did, I'd get bored halfway through. It would become a chore and I wouldn't finish it. I've often wondered why this happens. Once, for instance, I became passionate over Einstein's theory of relativity because of a picture I saw in my physics book. It was a drawing of a man on a bicycle going faster than the time around him —something like that. I had to know everything about relativity. I felt there was something in that little drawing that could change my life. I rushed out and bought some books on relativity and sat down with the feeling I was going to crack the secret at last. But within ten minutes I was bored to death. I seemed to have lost the impetus. Yet I could go back today and look at that same little drawing of the man pedaling faster than time and recapture the same excitement of being onto something."

"That happens all the time," said John, lacing his fingers. "Only people don't know why it's happened to them. But it's simple."

"What? Tell me!"

"It's because you're not pursuing the subject for itself," he said. "You're looking for something within it which speaks to your own need at that moment. It's easy to confuse that 'something' with the broader subject. If the subject goes flat, that's because you've gone beyond the point. You've swerved from your own, inner-dictated line of growth through a false allegiance to consistency."

"That's true, I hadn't thought of it. How clever of you, John." Polly looked at Dane as she said it: See, I *do* appreciate your husband. "But how do I get back on the track?"

"Go back to your man on the bicycle. What excited you may have had nothing to do with relativity."

"As a matter of fact, it didn't! It had to do with—oh, a certification that marvelous things did abound in the world, that average men could cycle completely out of the ruts which were their lives."

"You sound as though you're onto it again," encouraged John.

Dane quietly sipped her third gin and lime. She had been playing Robin's game and noting its advantages. When you didn't speak, then people were obliged to interpret your silence. And that was where it got interesting.

They usually interpreted it according to their own guilts or needs. Penelope, at the moment, was worried that Polly had seen that last yearning glance toward Karl; Polly was wondering if she'd made a fool of herself this afternoon; John was undecided: was his wife angry, feeling tired, sick, or had she had a new idea? And all she was doing was sitting there, a slight remote smile playing about her lips, registering the little red giant-white dwarf skit. Soon there would be dancing. She would watch that, too.

The French couple suddenly appeared out of the night. Luminous, poised, they drifted in their usual effortless harmony to a nearby table. He held her chair. Seated her. With his white long-sleeved shirt open at the neck, bending neatly from his narrow waist, he was graceful as a gypsy dancer. He consulted with her, then went off to the bar, nodding pleasantly to Karl and Count Bartolomé, who made a place for him. A select little trio of virility.

". . . one's vital interests are always good indications of where one's at," said John.

The Frenchwoman wore a fuchsia-colored jumpsuit of some soft, billowy material that echoed her movements. She opened a little beaded purse, took out a pack of American cigarettes, tamped one out, and lit it with a slim gold lighter. She inhaled. Dane watched the movement of her long, deeply tanned throat as it took the smoke. Her glossy black hair was brushed back from her face, the top-knot caught with a plain clasp. Any other woman would have sought to heighten the effect by wearing a matching fuchsia ribbon, thus drawing all the attention to her outfit and taking away from herself. It was a gift, thought Dane, just like a high IQ or musical ability: being able to move beautifully about the world as though it were your living room, diving into its green seas with no premeditation, bearing its children, wearing its fibers against your skin tanned by its sun. Watching this woman's natural grace as she simply sat, smoked her cigarette and waited for her husband to come back, Dane felt herself to be totally synthetic. What of the organic was in her?

One of the band plucked his electric guitar. The note, amplified by a loudspeaker, resounded richly across the patio.

"Dancing soon," said Penelope, sipping nervously at her drink. She knew Karl's every move. There was a bit of the organic about Penelope, but her nervousness and self-doubts marred it. Also, she was not as beautiful as the Frenchwoman.

What had they said to each other, down on the beach?

The band launched into "Guantanamera." The Frenchman returned to the table with two Pernods. Karl left the bar, calling something back to the Count. Penelope kept her eyes fast on her glass as he approached.

But he stood behind Dane's chair. "Will you dance?" he asked, amiably.

"Why not?" she said. She knew it for the gesture it was, but she wanted to dance with him and see if she found him sexy.

She couldn't decide. She liked his smell: a sort of minty one, out of a bottle, his own sort of war paint before the attack. He would be a practiced lover. He would do things for effect. He would practice smiles before his private mirror. But there was something deadly smooth about him as he led her into the music with him. They didn't speak. Once she looked at him rather sarcastically and found her look returned with a similar one. He was the sort of man who would take her to bed and torment her for being neither beautiful nor sincere. ("What do *you* know, little bluestocking? Let me show you a thing or two.") He was a good dancer and made her able to be one, too. She was beginning to lose herself in the dance when suddenly the music was over. Then she hated him, for she knew he would not ask her again.

Next he danced with his wife. They kept stopping in the middle of the music and talking. He laughed frequently. Penelope was in mortal agony.

When her turn came, she sulked at first, but Dane saw her soften as he turned his body to hers.

"Good photography in the offing, I think," said Dane.

Polly beamed, eternally grateful for this collaborator's remark.

"I think we should dance," John said to his wife.

"Sure, go on. I'll watch you," Polly said.

She rose, feeling she should.

It was all wrong from the start. When they reached the dance floor, the music stopped. Some people went back to their tables, others to the bar.

"Let's wait. It won't be long," John said. They stood at the edge of the dance floor. Dane was sure Count Bartolomé was watching them from his stance at the bar.

"Where do you think Polly is, on the circle?" she asked.

He thought a minute. "She's pretty positive tonight," he said. "I should say between 'Exploration' and 'Cooperation.'"

"Which is higher?"

"Cooperation."

"I don't agree."

"I know you don't." He laughed.

At last the band began to play. But it was some tricky rhythm. "I can't do that," she said. "Let's sit down."

"Let's try," he said. "What's the harm?"

Other couples filled the floor. The Frenchman and his wife were among them. They slipped into the odd rhythm at once, seeming to improvise as they went along.

John bumped into another couple. "Excuse me," he called over his shoulder. Dane could see Count Bartolomé's head swivel as he watched them curiously: So *that* is the father of that sad, strange little boy. She danced on tiptoe to keep her balance. Somehow, John was the wrong height for her. He should have been a half inch taller or shorter. As he was, she kept bumping against his stomach.

"Please, let's go back, John. I can't do it." They danced quite close to the bar. The Count was watching them openly, his boot hooked on the bar rail.

She tossed back her head and pretended to be having a marvelous time dancing with her husband. As soon as they were out of his line of vision, she said, "John, *please*."

"But we're getting better, don't you feel it? We can learn to do it."

"We'll never learn to do it. We don't move together. Our animals snarl at each other. No amount of *practice* can change that basic fact."

"Nonsense. You don't give it a chance. We can get beyond our animals snarling at each other. Sorry." He had trod on her toe.

"You—clumsy—" Tears of outrage sprang to her eyes. "Every step we take on this floor makes me detest you more."

His face went oddly remote, like a mask. "I see," he said. "Let's go and sit down."

"Quitting so soon?" said Polly of the bright eyes.

"My back was beginning to hurt," Dane said.

"Oh, too bad. I had so hoped you two might come for drinks at the villa afterward."

"Out of the question. I love you, Polly, but I love my bed more."

"I understand," said Polly cheerfully. "I wonder if Penelope would like to come. Neither Karl nor I are a bit tired. Karl could walk her home afterward."

"I'll insist that she go," said Dane.

Robin was sleeping in the glow of the bedside lamp, his face untroubled as an angel's. She felt beneath the sheet and gave a little cry of disgust.

"I'll do it if you'd rather not," said John. It was the first time he'd spoken since they left Pedro's.

"I'll do it. Go to bed."

"If you're sure," he murmured. Dropping his clothes in a heap, he climbed wearily into bed. His long naked body looked forlorn. She could see no trace of the mysterious stranger she'd met at Lady Jane's. With a heavy sigh, he turned away, balling himself up beneath the covers. He would write it out of himself tomorrow, putting their dance-floor asymmetry and her cutting remark in their proper places on the negative side of the circle. He would label them and take away their sting, then leap, light as a deer, back to meditations of the positive.

Stately, like a sleepwalker, she went into the bathroom. She scrubbed her face, creamed it, wiped off the cream, slapped on some cologne to bring the color to her cheeks. She brushed her teeth with the toothpaste that burned her mouth agreeably. She put on a wispy floor-length nightgown and brushed her hair until she heard it crackle. Gradually, the frown marks softened on her brow and she looked like a clean young girl, grooming herself for her first love.

She flicked off the light beside Robin's cot and stood for a while in the dark, listening to John, who had begun to snore. Her nostrils were assailed by the sour smell of the wet child. Down below, the sea breathed baby breaths into the little cove.

Then, possessed by a sudden, visceral need, she scooped him up in her arms and conveyed him to her own bed. She put him in first and climbed in beside him. She pulled the clean cool sheet over them both. Then she curved herself to the body of the damp, sleeping child.

Chapter
Fourteen

John went out before dawn, hurriedly, softly, as though to a secret appointment. His movements woke her. She opened her eyes as soon as he was gone.

The room was the gauzy gray of a specter. Ramón Lull smiled enigmatically from the dresser, the crude wooden features rather sinister. A rooster crowed. This was their last full day on the island. There was something of the no-man's-land about last days. They floated like smoke between past and future. They were not really there. The acrid odor of dried urine reminded her of Robin's presence in her bed. Her own nightgown was damp and smelly.

She must get up and rid the room of this stink. But she seemed unable to raise herself from the unpleasant bed. She dozed, again and again, among visions of how to begin the day. She dreamed the windows turned a reddish gleaming gold at the edges and heavenly music played and she leaped from bed, put on her swimsuit and ran down to the beach, plunging into the icy morning sea and swimming alone to meet the great orange sun god as it rose triumphant over the legions of dead. In another dream, she waked the child, sponged away his sourness, dressed them both in swimsuits and led him down to the beach. "Look, Robin. That is the sun coming out of the sea. Sun. Can you say it?" And his small, wondrous reply came: *"Sun."* And, in a third dream, she and Robin ran across the sand and up the hundreds of little stone steps which led to the Heykoop villa. Lighter than air, they skimmed those stairs to stand outside the villa and throw pebbles at the upstairs window with its billowing curtains until Polly's morning-sleepy face appeared in it. "If you still want to be friends, come down!" called Dane. And Polly's urchin face went radiant. "Don't move. I'll be right down!"

But then came the real clatter of cutlery from the dining room below, and the Spanish voices of the help, and the room had gone from reddish gold to plain morning yellow and the moment to have seized the day-that-might-have-been was past.

She flung herself from the disordered, smelly bed and cursed. The child moaned, dug his fist into the pillow, but went on sleeping.

She stripped his cot, filled the tub with water, dumped in the sheets. Must get the smell out. Who could wait for the maids, who took their own good time? She slipped him out of the pajamas and transferred him to his father's bed. Stripped her bed, threw the sheets and his pajamas in the tub, stepped hastily out of her own gown, threw that in. She dressed in the first thing she could find, saw John's heap of clothes on the floor, picked up the rust-colored terry cloth shirt and smelled it. Phew! Also, the collar was filthy. She ran to the bathroom and took a little bar of hotel soap and her nailbrush and began scouring the collar. When the label was immaculate, she filled up the washbasin with warm water and plunged in the rest of the shirt. She kneaded the shirt beneath the water and as she did she noticed her hairbrush lying on top of the basin. Dirty! She plucked out the hairs, dropping them in a bunch into the toilet. Flushed it. Scrubbed the bristles with the nailbrush. Discovered a dirty comb and washed that too. Then she had an idea: she would wash all their clothes, hang them to dry in this last day of hot Spanish sun, and they would go home with clean clothes. Back to the bedroom she went, plundering John's suitcase for soiled items, emptying their closet. She carried piles of shirts, shorts, little and big socks, pajamas, bras, handkerchiefs to the bathroom.

She washed these, one at a time, in the little washbasin, until the tiny bar of soap vanished in her reddened hands. Begrudging the time, she went out in search of the maids. She found them drinking coffee in the linen closet on the floor below.

"I need more soap," she said. "Soap. I am washing." She pantomimed a woman scrubbing at the sink.

One of them giggled. "Ah, *jabón!*" she said, rummaging in a cardboard box. She handed Dane another of the tiny bars, wrapped in paper.

"Excuse me, that's not enough. May I have more? *Más?* I am doing much washing." She made more vigorous washing gestures. Unsmiling, the maid gave her two more bars, rather dubiously.

"Stupid women," she muttered, taking two steps at a time back to the room. She washed every single item that was washable. When she came to the sheets, she did them, one at a time, in the tub, using the nailbrush. When she hung them out to dry with the other things, the sun already had a burn to it. She stood back and surveyed her work, but she was still unsatisfied. Damp strands of hair flew about her face. Her fingertips were numb and shriveled white from the water. With a feeling near to joy, she remembered her purse: it had not been cleaned out since her marriage. She hurried into the room, grabbed the purse, sat down on the cool floor with the waste-paper basket at hand.

Kleenex, stray hair clips, dried-up ballpoint, a single earring, keys to the magazine office and to her last pretty flat with the view of the riverboats, ticket stubs from the Chelsea Classic cinema the night they'd seen *Jane Eyre* and she'd cried all night for Rochester, a perfectly good pencil that had lost its point, a lipstick she was sure had belonged to Vanessa (she had found it fallen behind the dresser in John's room and had hoarded it for the day she might find a use for it), an old assignment book from her job (if she looked—which she didn't—she could see written in her own hand: *Mensa mting, Lady Jane Rotherhall, Bloomsbury Sq. @ 7:30*), swatches of various red materials for possible new curtains to improve John's living room (but there had been so much else wrong with it that she had given up and attacked the kitchen instead), one of John's handkerchiefs she had borrowed in a fit of sneezing and which should have been washed with the other stuff, some Jehovah's Witness literature someone had thrust on her in Piccadilly which she hadn't thrown away because she'd intended to read the article about a young man in Oxfordshire who'd had a religious experience, an Easter card from Mrs. Christopher, and the soiled tennis ball Mrs. Hart had sent Robin and which Dane had forgotten to give him . . .

Into the wastebasket with all of it.

She kept only her passport, international vaccination certificate and two crisp five-pound notes John had given her. There was a handful of troublesome halfpennies. She couldn't bring herself to throw away money and didn't want them to ruin the Spartan sanctity of her purse.

She was in the act of pouring them into a pocket of John's suitcase when he entered the room. The color was in his cheeks and his dark eyes sparkled. He looked about nineteen.

"I was just putting some halfpennies in your suitcase," she said, expecting him to laugh.

"Were you?" But he didn't even smile.

"Where did you go creeping off to this morning?"

"I went for a walk. I watched the sun come up, over the sea." She hated the self-righteousness of this statement.

"I washed all our things," she said.

"What things?"

"Oh, clothes, underclothes, your shirts, the sheets—"

"Wouldn't the maids have done the sheets?" He seemed awfully far away.

"Oh, I couldn't wait. The room. You could smell it a mile. I took him to my bed, his was so awful."

"Yes, I see."

"Where did you go to watch the sun rise?"

"To the end of the island to the little harbor. The fishermen were just returning. They gave me some coffee in an old mug. We stood around, drinking coffee, and the sun came up and it felt right."

"Well, I'm glad you made it to see your little harbor."

"Yes. I'm glad, too."

"Today is our last day," she said. "Have you forgotten your swim to the fort?"

"No, I hadn't forgotten."

"Can I still go with you?"

"You can. May. You'll do what you want."

"What did you mean when you said it 'felt right'? Was seeing the sun rise and standing there with the fishermen anything like your tree experience?"

He would not rise to the bait. "It meant something to me. What, I'm not sure. Perhaps if you'd been there, you would have felt it, too."

"Oh, dear. Missed out again, did I? Another moment of shared truth down the drain."

"How long has he been awake?" John asked, ignoring the other.

Robin lay wide-eyed, staring up at them. "I don't know," she said. "Since the beginning of time. I'd give anything to know what he thinks of us."

"Are you sure you'd want to know?" John said.

After breakfast, the French family left. The were standing in the lobby, dressed for travel, Ramírez-Suárez buzzing round them as though they were made of honey, when the Empsons came out of the dining room.

"I'll be up in a minute. I want to buy some postcards," Dane said to John.

She stationed herself at the postcard rack and slowly spun the little scenes of crowded beaches, lush foliage, cathedrals and much expanse of blue sea, looking beyond it all at the departing guests. Ramírez-Suárez said something about a taxi in French. The woman smiled charmingly and said, *'Merci.'* She wore a tan belted suit of raw silk and had knotted an orange paisley scarf about her neck. Her long legs in brown street shoes glowed mahogany. The children capered about, making a playroom of the lobby, but the parents had the remote look of people in transit to a better place.

The taxi came. The same sullen driver who was curt to John got out of his door and stood whistling in the driveway while the Frenchman and Ramírez-Suárez carried down the heavy luggage. The mother gave directions to the children, who clambered into the back seat. She and her husband put their heads together, discussed something. She got in beside the children. Ramírez-Suárez made sure her door was locked. The Frenchman shook Ramírez-Suárez's hand and passed him a folded bill. He got in the front seat with the driver and away they went.

Dane hurried upstairs. She didn't want to chat with Ramírez-Suárez. With the Frenchwoman's perfection gone, she felt a sudden relief. *She* was the only young, pretty mother staying at the Cala d'Or Hotel. But what was so great about the Cala d'Or Hotel? A sober, lackluster place where defeated Nazis and respectable widows came, summer after summer. The morning sun showed dust on the leaves of the potted palm on the landing. She wished to be gone from here also. They should have left today. The place was hers, uncontested by standards she couldn't meet, but it was an empty victory.

"Well, Penelope. Last day," she said. They lay side by side on the beach. Very few people had come down. Robin was constructing a new mound, frowning as he made his endless trips

242

to the water. "Are you resigned to Hatchard's on Monday?"

"Oh, *Hatchard's!*" moaned the girl. "Why did you have to bring that up?"

"Reality has a way of asserting itself. I suppose you'll be lonely at first."

"At first. I suppose I shall be. Until Karl comes."

"*Where* is he coming?"

"To London next month. To arrange for an exhibition. And"—she picked at a hangnail shyly—"to see me."

Dane laughed harshly. "For a minute there, I expected you to say you were getting married."

"Maybe we will someday," the girl said dreamily. "'Whatever will be, will be.'"

"Aren't you forgetting something?"

"That he's already married? No. But marriages have been known to break up."

"Theirs won't. It's solid as an old photograph album. You're only a page in it." And your time, marked in white ink, runs out today. What would Polly do? Tear out the page and do a fresh one? Use ink eradicator? Fly to London and hang upside down from the Hilton's flagpole to photograph them necking in Hyde Park?

"You're a gruff old thing. But I know it's because you are trying to protect me. You and John have been so clever, but, you know, I've found you out."

"What have you found out?"

"You didn't bring me here to cure me. You brought me here to show me I wasn't sick.

I'd simply lost the love of life. I'd forgot the pleasure of simple things: like horses, and sun, and flirting, and touching water. I'm not sick; London is. But if John had tried to tell me that when I was so depressed, I would have felt he was trying to chuck me out because I wasn't rich enough or interesting enough to take up his time. And you! Sly thing! All those cups of coffee. You were drawing me back into life."

"I'm touched that you see all this." Dane bared her teeth in a cryptic little smile. Penelope's exuberant voice sounded as though she were listening to it through a seashell. "By the way, I meant to ask you: do you speak any foreign languages?"

"Only French. I was Tartuffe in our school play. All girls. Why?"

"Then you and Karl will have to speak English." She had meant to worm from Penelope her conversation with the Frenchwoman, but suddenly lost interest.

"Oh, we shall communicate." Penelope laughed. "Besides, words take one only so far."

"True, true." She studied the small body of her stepson. His toes looked like ten tiny red sausages planted stubbornly in the sand. Those cocktail ones that you stuck a toothpick into and went *chomp*. Once she had read a story about a man who chopped off his wife's fingers, one by one, each time she lost a bet with him.

"Don't look now, but here comes Karl. Don't say I said anything about London, okay?"

"My lips are sealed."

He came across the sand like a big blond cat. "Good morning!" he called. He crouched between the two women. Dane sniffed the minty smell, could see him slapping his jaw with it before he came down to the beach.

"How is Polly?" she asked.

"Fine! She has taken the twins into Palma this morning. They are going to take pictures of Bellver Castle. I'll bet you didn't know my wife is a smashing photographer."

Dane laughed. "I'll bet I did." Penelope had gone rather sullen at his praise of his wife.

"You know what *we* are going to do today?" Karl nudged Penelope.

"Lady Godiva with clothes on." She brightened.

"That's right! I have arranged for you to have Serafina early this afternoon. All you have to do is enjoy your riding. Poor Karl will be down in the dust, trying to catch you with his crayons. Later, we will take the clothes off—in the painting," he amended for Dane's sake.

"Don't remind me," she said. "Off or on, it's all the same to me."

He looked at her curiously, shading his eyes from the sun. What had she said so outrageous? Was there something the matter with the way she looked?

"John is going to swim," said Penelope. They all squinted toward her husband, who was making his descent from the hotel. He wore his old maroon swim trunks and carried a white towel over his arm like a waiter. When he crossed the beach, his sandals kept getting bogged down with sand and he had to lift his feet unnaturally high. She hated the Dutchman for staring so blatantly at John's polio leg.

"Good morning, Doctor!" Karl called breezily, continuing to squat between the two women. "It looks like you are going for a swim."

"*That's* right." John might have been congratulating a retarded patient. He stood looming over them and she wished he had spent more time in the sun and less in his mind. "I'm going to swim out to the old fort and have a look around."

"The old fort?" Karl laughed incredulously.

"Ramírez-Suárez says it dates back to the Inquisition. One might find something interesting out there."

"You'll find broken bottles and garbage and—well!" Karl looked at the women. "Unmentionable items—that's all I shall say."

"We'll see," John replied cheerfully. He stood on the thin leg and reached down to unbuckle the other sandal. "Would anyone like to join me?" He bent inquiringly to Dane and took off his glasses and slipped them into his swimsuit pocket.

She looked down at the sand. Sand had so much silver in it. Incredible how it looked tan from a distance. The ocean seemed to come nearer, making a roaring in her ears, making it difficult to hear words.

Penelope said something about "cramp." John mustn't go alone, she was saying.

246

His hand went to his stomach, palm flat against its paleness. Its flesh had little pot-holes in it, like the backs of her thighs. ". . . two hours since breakfast," he said.

Standing above her. Waiting. She felt incapable of lifting her head and opening her mouth to form a "yes" or "no." If "yes," she'd find it tiring, boring, and yearn for shore. If "no," she'd watch him go and worry about what she was missing. Either answer made her lose. But if she did not answer, stayed very still . . . The sand looked inviting to touch. It would be nice to strain a handful, hour-glasswise, through her brown fingers. But she mustn't move. Any gesture might bear implicitly the weight of a yes or a no.

"Well then," he said amiably, "I'm off. Don't wait to have lunch. I don't know how long I'll be. Depends on what I find."

She sat unmoving, her eyes fixed on the winking sand. The top of her head was patted. His footsteps scrunched away.

When he had gone a safe distance, she raised blank, emotionless eyes to his departure. He marched into the shallows like a crusader, waded out waist-high, took a deep breath and crouched with a violent shudder until all but his head was submerged. For several moments, his arms agitated rhythmically below the surface. Then he pushed off with hearty splashing and inaugurated a sensible, long-term breast stroke toward the tiny island.

". . . taking a risk, going all that distance alone?" said Penelope.

"John likes to take chances." She tried to clear her ears by sticking her fingers in them and working them around. They had become stopped up.

"It's less than two miles," Karl told Penelope lightly. "You could swim it, if you wanted to."

"As a child, I was always preached to about cramps," Penelope said. "Dad made me promise never to swim too far out alone . . . ."

John: seized midway by cramp. Begins to sink. Who could reach him? There would be screaming (hers?) from the beach. Karl would flex his blond body, run importantly into the sea, arms revving up at once like propellers, flashing gold toward the victim (push him under for good if he reached him first?). Ramírez-Suárez's busy fingers, dialing madly, summoning patrol boats . . . Crowd gathering: peasants, servants, guests, out of hiding like wasps being smoked out. All would look out to sea, curiously, with a feeling of delicious terror in their throats. "He was an English doctor, here on holiday," one would say. The maids would moan and wring their hands and weep. "That's his wife, the tall woman. And his little boy. Look how she stands there, bearing up. It reminds you of a Greek tragedy." "She's American," another would say. "Ah! *Those* women have courage when their men are struck down. . . ."

The body: craggy features reposed in dignity, brown eyes sealed, long hands crossed like the knights on tombs. Brought back by boat. A fisherman's boat. Sedatives in her room. Mrs. Hart around the clock by her side. Ramírez-Suárez and Penelope stuffing Robin with candy and Cokes downstairs. "But what will the señora do?"

"I shall arrange for everything, my dear. I did it for Geoffrey and I shall do it again. One does what must be done. You are coming to stay with me, you and the little boy. I have an enormous house in the country with rooms crying out to be lived in again, and acres of trees and grass and orchard and a *good* school nearby which I'm sure we shall get him into (we'll have him four weks at Christmas, four weeks at Easter and six weeks in the summer, does the little chap worlds of good to be off on his own with the other boys, right at the start) and you and I shall have such fun. You'll be the daughter I never had. We'll go shopping for clothes—they make gorgeous things for you young creatures—and to matinees and concerts and take little trips to the Continent. And I'm sure we can teach you to ride. You'd enjoy it so. Leave everything to me, you dear sad girl."

Karl repeated, "Shall we?"

Dane thought: Yes, he has the eyes of a villain. He might be capable of pushing an enemy under. There were even tiny gold hairs on the fleshy part of his cheeks, near the bridge of the nose. "Shall we . . . what?" she said.

"Go up there, to the terrace, in the shade. Let me treat you ladies to an aperitif and we shall have ringside seats for the doctor's performance."

"You are sweet," said Penelope.

Dane allowed the Dutchman to pull her to her feet.

"He is a man of few words," Karl said. "Tell me, blue-eyes, can you say your name?"

Robin, sitting on his pillows at their terrace table, frowned at the inquisitor. Dane prepared her usual speech about his shyness, but the words flagged, somewhere between thinking and saying them. She stared at the auburn of the Dubonnet, which Karl had chosen for her because she could not think what to order.

"He keeps himself to himself," said Penelope.

"Very astute," said Karl. One of his hands disappeared beneath the table. Penelope, in the midst of sipping her drink, gave a surprised little flush.

"How is your Dubonnet?" Karl asked Dane politely. His upper arm flexed as the lower, hidden part moved back and forth under the table. He made her feel a hundred.

"Quite fine," she said. Those were not the words she wanted.

John was over halfway to the fort. His dark head bobbed up and down in the smooth sea, no bigger than an insect making its laborious way across a light-green Formica tabletop.

Robin made a grunting noise. He leveled his small right index finger at the carafe of water in the center of their table. His cool eyes sought Dane's.

She returned the stare.

". . . early afternoon light is best," explained Karl to Penelope, "because it has strength *and* some shadows."

Now Robin set up a series of small stabbing motions with his finger toward the carafe. His eyes became imperious. The tip of the little finger was so red, as if all his blood had gathered just there in that one spot. Prick it with a pin and it would come gushing out in torrents. . . .

She went on watching him, transfixed, while an alternate self sighed, gave in, poured water into a glass and slid it across to calm the demanding little finger.

He sounded an opening note for his famous scream. Penelope and Karl now looked. He stabbed again and again at the carafe and his eyes demanded Dane to get moving.

"The man of few words wants water, I think," said Karl. "Is it what you want, old fellow?"

Robin fastened his eyes on the Dutchman and nodded once.

"He never asks," Penelope explained knowingly. "When he wants anything, he just points."

"*I* see." Karl's hidden hand emerged from beneath the table and traveled toward the carafe.

"Stop," Dane said. "Don't do that." Her voice was different. Very faraway, detached. "If he wants it, he must ask."

"But—" began Penelope.

Dane confronted Robin. The others faded

into a blur. Peripheries vanished. The universe consisted of herself and this child. The two pairs of blue eyes engaged. "If you want that water, you will have to ask for it," she said.

He glared at her. The eyes went hard with fury. The stiff red fingertip insisted on its object. The little shoes began to beat a rhythm of protest against the chair.

She said in the deadly calm new voice: "If you want it, you must say, 'Mommy, I want some water.' You can say it. Say 'Mommy, I want some water.'"

From deep in the child's throat, the siren noise began.

"Oh dear, he's going to cry," said Penelope. "Why not give it to him just this once?"

"Why not!" agreed the Dutchman. Both of them watched her as though *she* were the child about to make a scene.

"No," said Dane tonelessly. "Not until he asks."

He paused for full breath and let loose with a blood-curdling scream. Faces jerked round, masks of curiosity. She was isolated by a soft layer of purpose against their probing eyes.

"Not until you ask," she said.

His face went terrible with rage. He stopped being a child and became a small red shrieking obstruction. The shrieks launched her from her chair, lighter than helium.

"What are you going to do?" Penelope asked nervously.

"Take him upstairs and spank him."

"Why not wait until the doctor returns?"

Karl suggested in the conciliatory singsong one might use on a dangerous person. "My wife always waits for me to come home and do the smacking," he explained to Penelope.

"The hell she does," Dane said. She lifted the kicking, screaming body from its chair, the single index finger continuing to twitch imperiously toward the carafe. One thrashing foot caught the Dubonnet glass and set it smashing to the tiles. A flustered waiter hurried forward with a sponge. She slung the wild thing over her hip and floated into the hotel, taking the steps effortlessly. Everywhere, faces: like dumb pink flowers.

Ramírez-Suárez rushed toward her in the lobby. "He has hurt himself, señora?"

"He has been very bad," she said, not stopping. Up the stairs she went. The young manager remained below, watching their ascent, his hands outstretched in a gesture of bewilderment.

She closed the door of the bedroom and dumped him on his cot screaming. "We'll see who talks," she said. Her head felt effervescent, as if the brains had been replaced by ginger ale.

With a feeling of anticipation, she sat down on his cot. He lay as he had landed, screaming up at her, directing his screams as though, sooner or later, one would shatter her. For some moments she watched, fascinated as the little face poured forth the noise. Then she whisked him to her, pulled down the little yellow swim trunks and turned him across her knee. The taut translucent globes of his buttocks rose up before her eyes. She smacked one of them experimentally and a warm wetness flooded her mouth.

He yelled in amazement and pain.

She smacked again, getting them both, and again and again and again until his screams, her hand, the soft pliant bottom were parts of a single machine working together. She beat him until his tears soaked her lap and her hand stung from the peppery hotness of the inflamed little globes.

She paused for breath, then beat with the other hand. The screaming took on a plaintive, monotonous note. Then she plucked him from her knees and slammed him, face up, on his pillow. Thrusting her face within inches of his own crimson one, she said, "Are you going to say it?"

The child's bloodshot eyes locked with hers. Beyond the fear, the pain, there was a kind of superior scorn. Even as she began to hit his face, surprised at the silkiness of the touch, she knew he would never say it. And she became strangely pleased because it gave her the right to go on hitting that arrogant little face which had denied her for so long.

"Say it," she chanted. "Say it: 'Mommy, I want some water, Mommy, I want some water,'" her own voice an imitation of a little child's.

He gave her a look of pure negation and opened his mouth to scream some more.

"God damn you." She clamped her mouth down upon his and pressed with all her strength. A wonderful liquid feeling was set off in her womb and began coursing slowly toward her legs. She pushed her lips against his small milk-white teeth until she tasted her own blood. He struggled like a trapped animal but she held him down with her body, with her hands, with her mouth, drinking the sweet breath until she could get her fill.

She came to herself in pure, perfect peace. Her ears had cleared miraculously, and she could hear the sound of the sea below. Beneath her exhausted body, he had stopped struggling. His mouth, bruised and bloodied but freed at last, was busy taking urgent congested gasps.

When she could gather her energies, she crawled from the small form, looking down at the mottled face at just the precise moment when the blue eyes hardened against her in a decision far beyond their years. She slid from the cot and made her way, dazed, toward the closed doors leading to the balcony. The hollow eyes of Ramón Lull watched her impassively from the dresser.

She opened the doors and stumbled into the brilliant noon sun. Light flooded the island. There was not a shadow anywhere. The little beach buzzed with brown bodies and silver sand and a thousand tiny sounds. The sea glittered, lively as the green eye of a serpent.

"I almost killed him," she would say, when he returned from swimming the miles and fingering the secrets of the Inquisition.

Far out, on the tiny island, a pale speck crested with dark hair climbed out of the water. It paused on its forked body, flexed itself and turned back toward the hotel, shielding its eyes.

"Some force came over me, bigger than I was," she would say, possessed at last of some cosmic vision of her own.

"What was it like?" he would ask.

"It was powerful—and private. I'm sorry. I really can't tell you more than that. It was the sort of experience that can't be shared by anyone."

"But someone did share it," he would say, reestablishing the infernal balance.

"Bastard," she said aloud, squinting out to sea from the balcony.

The pale figure raised its arm and waved. Then it turned away and clambered eagerly over the rock toward the crumbling ruins of the old fort.